Fly With Me

Julie Hahn

To Eva,
May your life be
full of Adventure!
♡ Julie Hahn

Immortal Works LLC
1505 Glenrose Drive
Salt Lake City, Utah 84104
Tel: (385) 202-0116

© 2021 Julie Hahn
http://authorjuliehahn.com/

Cover Art by Ashley Literski
http://strangedevotion.wixsite.com/strangedesigns

ISBN 978-1-953491-08-4 (Paperback)
ASIN B08XV1YG73 (Kindle Edition)

To my loving and supportive husband and children, without whom this book would have been finished much sooner.

To all survivors, caretakers, and medical professions who battle against cancer every day, especially my sister, Becky, a courageous cancer survivor and the inspiration for this story.

Chapter 1

"What about this one, Jessa?" Mom showed me another shirt off the thrift store rack. No stains or holes, it didn't look worn or faded. Scrawled across the front in cursive, the brand name glittered in gold.

"Could be worse." I tossed it in the cart. "Why do we have to do our back-to-school shopping here?" My gaze drifted toward the glass doors at the front of the store. A mere thirty-minute drive and we could be at the mall.

"I'm sorry, *mijita*," she said, "but this is all we can afford right now."

"Can we buy at least one new shirt from the mall?" I gave Mom the puppy dog eyes that Dad couldn't resist.

Mom ignored me and kept looking through the shirts. "Sorry. Sarah and Kate still need their clothes. We don't have enough money to get the whole family new clothes."

"Please, mamá?"

"Why do you care so much? We shop here every year for school, and every year we find cute clothes for affordable prices." She pulled out a periwinkle shirt with the original tag still attached. "See? Brand new." She smiled at me and tossed it in the basket. "What's different this time?"

"It's the first day of *middle school*. I'll be meeting a ton of new kids. Please," I begged again. Mom didn't look up.

"What do you think of this dress?" She held up a cute floral maxi dress. "All your dresses are too small. This should last for a few years. And you can wear it to Mrs. Black's funeral tonight."

"It's cute," I responded. "The mall has a bunch of cute dresses too."

Mom chuckled but kept browsing.

The bell on the door jingled and in walked my best friend, Alexa, looking sun-kissed and tanned. Right behind her came a blonde girl with milky white skin whom I didn't know. I hadn't seen Alexa since school got out. I rushed over through the maze of clothing racks so we arrived at the counter at the same time. They each held a trash bag that they set on the floor. The blonde girl gave me a once-over before she turned to give the donation to the store clerk.

Alexa hugged me tight. "I've missed you so much this summer!" she squeed. I hugged her back. "I still wish you could have come with me. Camp Yogi would have been better with you there."

"Did you have fun? Tell me everything." My words came out in a rush. I'd never gone to summer camp before.

"A-mazing." She let go of me and tucked her short, golden brown hair behind her ears. "We did meditation at the lake before breakfast. And I took all sorts of cool yoga classes and activities." She held up a brand-new iPhone. "Look what I got for my birthday!"

"Wow! I'm jealous. Mom won't let me have one for another few years. Sarah just got her first phone, and she's almost sixteen," I lamented. "I still have to use the kids' phone."

"Ahem." The blonde girl cleared her throat.

"Oh! I forgot." Alexa blushed. "Carleigh, this is my best friend, Jessa." Alexa gestured to me. "And Jessa, this is Carleigh. She was my best friend at camp."

I smiled and held my hand out while my insides twisted. *Best friend?*

Carleigh didn't take it. Instead she gave me a skeptical look appraising my outfit. "Are you *shopping* here?"

"I was, um, donating. Just finished." I shifted my feet, trying to hide the grass stains on my pink shoes. My older sister Sarah's hand-me-down shirt hung loose on me.

Carleigh raised her eyebrows. "Right." Her tone said she didn't believe me. She turned to Alexa. "When we're done here, do you want to go get a green smoothie?"

"Of course." Alexa gave me a slight shrug.

I smiled to let her know my feelings weren't hurt.

"Jessa, are you ready to go?" Mom pushed a cart full of clothes over to us.

I could feel the blush rising from my toes all the way to my forehead.

"Donating, huh?" Carleigh raised an eyebrow at me.

Alexa cleared her throat and looked away.

"Hi, Lexi, did you have a good summer?" Mom gave Alexa a half hug. "We missed seeing you at the house." Mom started pulling clothes out of the cart and putting them on the counter. "Who is your new friend?"

Carleigh smiled and held her hand out to Mom. "Hi, you must be Jessa's mom. I've heard a lot about Jessa from Alexa."

Mom smiled and shook Carleigh's hand. "Nice to meet you."

"She went to Lincoln Academy," Alexa said.

I died a little inside. Of course, Carleigh attended the snootiest private school around.

"Went to?" Mom asked.

"My mom wants me to get a more"—Carleigh paused as she searched for the right word—"*common* social upbringing so she's sending me to Sunnyside Middle this year." She scrunched her nose as though the thought of going to a public middle school smelled bad.

"You'll be starting sixth grade with Jessa?" Mom asked.

Carleigh nodded.

"How fun." The enthusiasm in Mom's voice sounded genuine. She turned to the cashier and started piling my "new" clothes on the counter.

"Who's your homeroom?" I asked Alexa.

"Carleigh and I both have Mr. Black," Alexa said.

"Me too!" I squeed.

"I can't believe he's not taking time off after his wife died," Mom muttered.

I elbowed her gently. "Let's not talk about Mrs. Black right now," I begged. Mrs. Black died in her sleep a week ago, and it seemed like the only thing any adult wanted to talk about.

"Sorry, it's just so sad. They were about to take their second honeymoon. She told me they'd already booked the tickets to Paris." Mom added the last few items to the pile on the counter.

My cheeks flashed with warmth. Why was she so embarrassing? "Mom, seriously," I pleaded.

Mom turned her attention to the cashier, and Alexa changed the subject. "Are you coming to my party on Friday? We can compare the rest of our schedules if you come a little early."

I hesitated, hating that I needed to get Mom's permission in front of Alexa and Carleigh, before looking over at Mom. "She can go if she gets her chores done," Mom said, giving me a pointed look.

Carleigh coughed, but it sounded more like a laugh to me.

"Who else is coming?" I asked Alexa.

"I'm bringing all the best kids from Lincoln," Carleigh answered instead, then turned toward Alexa. "I can't wait for you to meet Anna. She'll be at Sunnyside this year too. You'll absolutely love her." She looped her arm through Alexa's and started walking toward the door. "She totally reminds me of Sophie—"

"—from Cabin B?" Alexa asked as she opened the door. She didn't even glance back at me.

"What's in these bags?" Mom asked, indicating the trash bags Carleigh had donated.

"No," I said, trying to sound firm.

Mom gave me a questioning look before nodding and paying for my clothes.

I wouldn't be caught dead wearing Carleigh's hand-me-downs to school, even if they were cute.

My soft, new maxi dress flowed down to my toes. I was glad when Mom suggested I wear it to the funeral. Mom had a strict, no-wearing-new-school-clothes-before-school-starts policy.

I stood in line at Mrs. Black's viewing with Mom and Sarah. Alexa stood a few spots ahead of us in line. Her mom shook Mr. Black's hand while Alexa played on her new phone. She didn't even look up when the line moved her to the casket.

Mom squeezed my hand, and I squeezed back as we took another step toward the casket. We were next in line to shake Mr. Black's hand and tell him sorry his wife had died. Sorry didn't seem like enough.

Mrs. Black had been my fifth-grade teacher last year. Her class had been my favorite so far. She'd filled her room with quotes from *Peter Pan* and even had a stuffed Captain Hook doll that sat on her desk.

We took another step forward. Did I want to see her like this? Would she look the same? From where I stood, I could see a bit of her pretty brown hair.

"We're sorry for your loss." Mom shook hands with Mr. Black.

"Thank you, Mrs. Newberry." He patted Mom's hand.

My turn.

I reached my hand out and he took it with his cold, dry hands.

"I'm glad you came, Jessa." The tie tack, pinned to his red tie, flashed gold in the light. He smelled like peppermint gum. "You were one of Caroline's favorite students."

I nodded and pulled my hand away. I had never heard her called Caroline before. "I-I'm sorry," I stammered, trying but failing to imitate Mom.

Sarah shook his hand after me, then Mom pulled me gently until we moved forward, in front of the casket.

Mrs. Black's face looked fake, covered in too much makeup. Her eyes were closed and the smile lines on her face were gone. She looked almost waxy. I shuddered. She looked wrong.

"She looks peaceful," Mrs. Johnston said as she and Alexa walked away from the casket.

We could only see the top half of her body. She wore a white dress and a pretty necklace. Her hands were arranged on her torso and her wedding ring sparkled on her finger. *Would they bury her with her jewelry on? Did she have shoes on?*

Mom pulled my hand and we walked away. Sarah took a small package of tissues from her purse and handed them to mom. The other guests were dabbing their eyes as they spoke in hushed tones.

Was there something wrong with me? Sure, I was sad, but why wasn't I crying?

I COULDN'T SLEEP that night. An image of Mrs. Black with waxy, pale skin kept floating to the surface of my mind.

After tossing and turning for hours I opened my eyes, to check the clock. My room had transformed. Around me my walls had faded to rough-hewn logs. I stood in a tree house bigger than my bedroom. Several patched, dust-covered cloth hammocks hung from posts around the room. Light streamed through the door and several windows. Out of one window I could see a bright blue ocean and a sandy beach.

A long ladder led down the trunk to the forest floor fifty feet below. A flash of white among all the green and brown caught my attention. I started climbing down the damp ladder rungs to investigate.

The muggy air smelled like rain and made my hair stick to the back of my neck. I'd been climbing for a while but when I looked down, the ground wasn't any closer. My sweaty hands and feet were slippery on the rungs. I gripped them tighter. The urge to get my feet on the ground pushed me onward. I kept climbing down, stopping every few minutes to shake the fatigue from my arms. The ground still hadn't come any closer. I looked up and the tree house seemed as distant as the ground. Why couldn't I get down?

My foot slipped and the world flew past in a whirl of green and brown. Branches and vines whipped my face. My hands scrambled to grab hold of anything to slow my fall but grasped only leaves. I squeezed my eyes shut, wishing I could fly.

My fall stopped. My breath came fast. Nothing hurt. Had I hit the ground? I opened my eyes to see the ground a foot below me. Somehow, I hovered in the air.

Impossible.

The ground rushed up and knocked the wind out of me. I rolled to my back and tried to suck in air. After a long minute of gasping, I was able to sit up. A light layer of leaves and pine needles covered the forest floor. I brushed them off me as I stood.

I heard a rustling to my left and turned toward it.

"Are you okay?" a woman's voice asked.

"Mrs. Black?" She looked the same, but different—younger, slimmer. A soft golden light surrounded her.

"Jessa, I'm happy to see you." Mrs. Black gave me a warm smile.

I stepped away from her and her smile faded.

"Are you okay?" she asked, her eyebrows drawing together. "You look like you've seen a ghost."

"I have. I mean...you're dead. I went to your funeral today." Mom would have chided my bluntness. "Sorry."

Mrs. Black smiled, but in a sad way. "I know." She stepped forward and touched my shoulder; her vanilla scent enveloped me. "It's been quite a transition, but I'm always up for an adventure."

This was so weird. She felt real, though, and she smelled the same. I kept my eyes trained on the ground. I couldn't look at her alive now when a few hours before she'd been pale and cold in her casket.

Her eyes looked sad. "I hope Jim is okay," she muttered, more to herself than to me. "He's never been good on his own." She looked out at the canopy of trees toward the sunset.

"I think it's time for me to go now."

"Go where?"

She gave me a sad smile. "Home ... of sorts. I can't stay here much longer. This place isn't for me."

"What do you mean?" I asked, but too late. Her whole being shimmered and brightened like sunlight reflecting off water.

I closed my eyes and turned my head away. A hot breeze blew past my face. I opened my eyes. I was back in my room and Mrs. Black was gone.

Chapter 2

The next day, after I'd finished my chores and mowed the lawn, I took a quick shower and got dressed for the party.

I dried my hair and tried a braid, but it didn't turn out. I opened Sarah's drawer to borrow the straightener Mom bought her. Sarah wouldn't be happy about it, but she didn't have to know. Of all three girls, only Sarah had inherited Mom's thick, dark hair, and Mom went to great lengths to help her take care of it. My mousy brown hair was thin by comparison.

I straightened it as fast as I could. Sarah and Mom had taken my little sister, Kate, to karate class, which lasted a half an hour, so they would be back any minute. As I put it away, I noticed a headband Sarah hadn't worn for years, stuffed in the back. I pulled it out. It looked like it was the same shade of periwinkle as the shirt from the thrift store. I found the bag of clothes, pulled out the shirt, and tried it on. The colors matched well enough that they looked like a set.

I needed to wear something to the party other than last year's ratty clothes. I'd have to figure out how to sneak it out without Mom seeing it.

I jumped as the door opened and Sarah walked in. Her long hair flowed down to her waist. She looked me up and down. I held my breath as I scooted past her into the hall.

"Is that *my* headband?" she asked, when I made it to the doorway.

I stepped out of her reach. "Please can I borrow it?" I said, keeping my voice low so Mom wouldn't hear us from downstairs. "You have all the cute stuff. All of mine look like they should belong to Kate, and unlike Kate I'm not six."

She glanced at her open drawer where I'd put the straightener before giving me a scrutinizing look. "Why are you wearing new school clothes?"

"I was just trying this shirt on." I took another step away from her as my hand reached up and touched the headband. "It's a perfect match."

"If you were just trying it on, why do you want to borrow my headband?"

I didn't respond.

"Jessa?" Her voice held a warning in it.

"Please?" I begged. I glanced down toward the kitchen. "Don't tell Mom."

Sarah moved toward me. Her lips formed a thin line. Her hand stretched out to rip the headband off me but before she could reach me, I turned and ran into my room, slamming the door behind me.

She pounded on my door. "Give it back."

"C'mon, I can't wear baby bows. And you don't even wear headbands anymore."

The pounding stopped. "Give it back or I'll tell Mom what you're wearing." She said in a smug tone. She knew she'd won.

I pulled the headband off, opened the door, flung it at her, and slammed the door again.

"Who is slamming doors up there?" Mom shouted.

"It's just Jessa. She's stealing my stuff," Sarah called. "And she's trying to wear her new school clothes to the party tonight."

"Jessa!" Mom called. "Get down here."

I opened the door to a smirking Sarah. I glared at her and muttered "Jerk," as I passed.

DAD PULLED up to Alexa's ten minutes early. The kids' phone sat like a brick in my pocket.

"Text me the code if you want to leave before the party ends. Otherwise I'll come get you at 8:30," Dad said as I exited the car. "Do you remember the code?"

I rolled my eyes and turned to face him. "If something makes me uncomfortable, send you a text with the letter 'X' and you'll drop everything to come and get me." I gave him my best smile. "I don't think I'll have to worry about that tonight. It's Alexa."

Dad nodded. "You never know." He tapped his cheek for a kiss but I did not want to kiss him. What if someone saw?

I hesitated long enough.

"Too cool to kiss your old man?" he asked.

I held my fist out and he gave me a fist bump, then I shut the car door and headed up the path to Alexa's giant house. Butterflies fluttered around in my stomach as I rang the doorbell.

The butterflies turned to knots when the door opened. Carleigh stood there, dressed in shimmery white and gold leggings and a wide-neck mint top. Her long blonde hair wound around her head in intricate braids that led to a bun on top of her head. She looked casual and chic at the same time.

I cringed at my worn sneakers and jeans with holes in the knees. My faded shirt had a print of a cat, cracked with age and peeling off. It was the best I could find after Sarah tattled on me and Mom made me change. At least my jeans didn't have grass stains on them.

"Hey, Jessa." She pulled the door open for me to enter, then walked off.

I hesitated for a moment before I stepped inside. Why was

Carleigh here before the party started? Had they been hanging out all day?

I slipped my shoes off and left them by the door. By the time I made it into the kitchen Carleigh stood next to Alexa who held a pink highlighter. They hovered over the counter, shoulder to shoulder, looking at their schedules. Alexa and I used to match up our sports or summer schedules. She always used pink highlighter to mark our team's soccer games, the summer classes we wanted to take together, or even the free time when we could hang out.

"We both have gym last period. I'm so relieved," Alexa said as she marked both papers.

Why did Carleigh get the pink highlighter?

"Yeah, we don't have to be sweaty all day," Carleigh said. Did Carleigh even sweat? She seemed like the kind of person who didn't.

Alexa looked up and grinned. She ran over and gave me a quick hug. "Did you bring your schedule?" she asked, leading me to the table. I pulled it out of my back pocket and set it next to hers.

She leaned over and started talking. "Let's see; we have fourth period science together and English with Mr. Black first period. Buuut"—she dragged the word out as she marked our shared classes with a yellow highlighter—"I don't think we have any other classes together."

I looked down at the papers. I had gym second period. Great. I'd have to be the smelly, sweaty kid all day or shower at school. I didn't know which was worse.

Alexa slid my schedule back to me and grimaced. "This sucks. I was hoping we'd have all our classes together."

"We all have fourth period science. That means we all have A lunch," Carleigh said.

"At least we can hang out during lunch break," Alexa said.

I looked at Carleigh's schedule. Pink highlighter covered both of their schedules, marking the classes they shared. "Do you have all your classes together?" I asked.

"All but one," Alexa grinned. "I'm taking keyboarding and Carleigh is taking art. Otherwise our schedules match exactly."

"I have sixth period art, too," I pointed out.

"At least you'll know someone in there," Alexa said and Carleigh shrugged.

The doorbell rang and Alexa and Carleigh went together to answer it. I followed behind them and got there as they let in five girls whom I didn't know.

"Alexa, these are my best friends from Lincoln. This is Anna." Carleigh pointed to a girl with straight black hair that fell to her waist. "She's coming to Sunnyside this year too."

Anna gave Alexa a tight smile. She didn't look pleased about having to change schools.

I hung back, thinking Alexa or Carleigh would introduce me, but right after all the Lincoln girls came in, a few of the popular boys from my class came in. And after they closed the door, another bunch of kids dressed in black rang the doorbell.

I stepped back into the kitchen as guests filed in until the house felt full. As everyone settled in, Alexa stayed with Carleigh and her Lincoln friends.

"Jessa!" a boy named Michael called from across the room. "How was your summer?" He was about my height, with dark russet skin, and warm brown eyes. He held out a hand for me to grab and pulled me into half a hug.

"Pretty normal." I shifted my focus from Alexa to Michael. He and I had never been good friends, but we'd been in the same class every year since preschool, so we knew each other pretty well.

"Do you have your schedule? We need to see if the tradition continues."

I pulled my schedule from my back pocket and he snatched it from my hand.

"Wow, we have almost all our classes together," he said from behind my schedule.

"Really? Let me see yours."

Michael tapped his temple. "Mine is all up here. But look"—he lowered the paper for me to see—"First period, Mr. Black. Second period, gym. You'll be with the girls so we probably won't see each other..."

I looked up at the sound of my name from somewhere in the crowd. I let Michael keep talking as I tried to home in on who had said it. It sounded like Carleigh.

There she stood by the door with her Lincoln friends and Alexa. They hadn't noticed me looking.

Had I heard wrong? After a few seconds, I realized they'd all stopped talking and were staring back at me and Michael. Anna made a kissing face, and they all erupted into giggles. Alexa blushed, and gave Anna a light push on her shoulder. Carleigh raised her eyebrows at me.

Heat swept through my body. I tore my schedule from Michael's hands and started to walk away.

"Are you okay?" he asked.

I didn't have the courage to look into his face. Instead, I kept my eyes trained on the ground and muttered, "Not feeling well. Bathroom," before I pushed past him and down the hall.

The bathroom door was locked so I headed to Alexa's room to lie down. Silence filled the dark room. I crawled onto her bed, letting the stillness envelop me. I squeezed my eyes shut. Why had I let those girls get to me? It's not like they were going to come to Sunnyside. They were Carleigh's friends from Lincoln, not my friends or Alexa's friends. I wouldn't see any of them again.

I opened my eyes and took a few breaths. I hadn't been in

Alexa's room all summer. Most of her stuff was the same. The usual two pictures of us sat on her dresser, but she'd added a third.

I stood and moved to the dresser to study the pictures. In the first picture, kindergarten me, Alexa, and a girl named Sidney Thatcher all stood under a tree modeling our matching rainbow shirts. The words *Best Friends* were written on our left sleeves. In the next picture Alexa and I stood side by side with an arm slung around the other's shoulder. Mom took this picture on the first day of school last year. In the last picture, Carleigh and Alexa both held a yoga pose and wore their matching Camp Yogi shirts.

I couldn't lose Alexa to Carleigh. I'd have to figure out a way to get along with her. After all, Alexa would do the same for me.

I CAME out of Alexa's room to see her singing karaoke with Anna and a few of the Lincoln girls. Carleigh stood near the food table munching on a carrot. I grabbed a plate and started loading chips and cookies on to it.

"This party is getting boring," Carleigh said. She tossed her plate in the garbage and picked up her almost-empty soda bottle. "Want to help me spice it up?"

The Karaoke music changed to a new song. Michael and two other boys were doing a terrible job of singing a '90's song. But they laughed and had fun instead of being embarrassed.

I shrugged. "I'm having fun."

She sighed and finished off her drink. "Let's play Spin the Bottle," she said, holding up the now empty bottle. "But I'm only going to invite the cool kids. I don't want to end up kissing a dork." She glanced over at Michael and his friends.

My fingers felt cold. I didn't want to play Spin the Bottle. I didn't want to kiss anyone yet, but had she called me a cool kid?

Carleigh found Anna and whispered in her ear. Anna smiled and nodded. She turned to a cute boy sitting near her and whispered in his ear. Carleigh nodded for me to follow as she walked into the front room

"Help me make some space." She scooted a chair toward the wall to make more room on the floor.

My stomach fell down to my shoes. Were they really going to play Spin the Bottle? I didn't want to play. Alexa came in looking excited but nervous, followed by three of the Lincoln girls and five of the cutest boys from school.

"We're going to play Spin the Bottle. Who's in?" Carleigh asked.

All the boys and the Lincoln girls scrambled to find a spot on the floor. Alexa hung back next to me.

"Are you going to play?" I whispered to her.

"Are you?" she whispered back.

"Our parents would kill us," I whispered.

Carleigh looked up at the two of us. "Are you playing or not?"

"I don't know," I hedged.

Carleigh scoffed. "Okay." She turned toward Alexa. "What about you?"

Alexa gave me a quick glance before she pushed past me and sat down next to Carleigh.

Had someone turned the heat up? My skin prickled with sweat. Everyone stared at me.

The phone buzzed in my pocket. I pulled it out to stall for time. Dad had texted me.

I'm outside, come when you're ready.

Relief flooded through me as I checked the time. 8:15. Dad's habit of showing up fifteen minutes early had *finally* worked to my advantage.

"My dad is here. I've gotta go." I slipped my shoes on trying to not make eye contact with anyone.

Anna and Carleigh shared a look.

"See you tomorrow," Alexa called.

I gave her a small wave and stepped out the door. The hot, sticky air almost took my breath away but compared to the pressure inside the house, it felt welcoming and free. The sun had set, and Venus shone bright above the horizon.

"Was it a fun party? A furty... No! A farty!" Dad asked after I climbed into the car. He looked at me the way he did whenever he wanted me to validate his latest combination. He loved coming up with portmanteaus—combining two words into one.

"What? A farty?" I asked. "Really?"

"Yeah, that's not a good one." He put the car into gear and pulled away from Alexa's house.

"Did you have fun?"

I shrugged, thinking of the last few minutes of the party. "Yeah, I guess." Had Alexa already had her first kiss? I closed my eyes and replayed the party scene. I couldn't figure Carleigh out.

"Hey, kiddo." Dad's voice wavered a little as he spoke. He cleared his throat. "Do you remember Sidney Thatcher?" He looked at me through the rear-view mirror.

"Sure." I half listened. I couldn't stop thinking about the end of the party.

"She had cancer, remember?" Dad asked. He was trying to tell me something important so I shifted my focus from the party to the current conversation.

"Yeah. We were pretty good friends, but I didn't see much

of her after she got sick." I thought of the picture on Alexa's night stand with the three of us.

"She's relapsed again." He cleared his throat again and his next words came out sounding like he had a head cold. "It's not looking good for her. I don't know if she'll make it through this time."

"Oh," I said. The party seemed less of a big deal. I hadn't talked to her in years, but the thought of her dying made me feel emptier inside.

"She could use a friend." Dad sniffed. "You should reach out to her." Dad always wanted to include everyone, defend the defenseless, and stand up for what was right. "Just be her friend. I'm sure she's lonely."

I didn't respond. It sounded awkward. Maybe if I knew Sidney better it'd be easier. What do you say to someone you haven't talked to in years who might be dying?

Chapter 3

Mom stood at the kitchen sink, just finishing up the dishes as we walked in. "How was the party?" she asked me.

I wasn't ready to talk about Spin the Bottle with anybody yet. "Um, it was okay." I grabbed a yogurt from the fridge and sat down at the bar to eat it.

"Is Kate in bed?" Dad asked.

Mom sighed, and wiped her hands on a towel. "Not yet. We had a slight difference of opinion on the subject. I asked her to go to bed and she started crying and yelling."

"What was wrong?" Dad asked.

"I don't know for sure. Best guess is she's anxious about school. I told her to go calm down on the patio and she could stay up until you got home."

"I'll go get her," Dad said.

"Let me get her," I said, finishing my yogurt and dropping the spoon into the sink. "I don't mind."

"Oh, is this one of those times when you think sisterly love is more powerful than fatherly love?" my dad asked, winking at me.

"Come on, Dad. When was the last time *you* had a first day of school? Forty years ago?" I winked back. "Mine was last year."

Dad laughed.

"Thanks, Jessa," Mom said.

I walked out the sliding glass door in the living room and saw Kate sitting on our favorite patio chair, with her knees pulled up to her chest and her head down.

"Hey, *chiquita.*" I said, squatting down next to her. *"¿Qué te pasa?"*

She looked up at me and her tear-filled eyes shone in the moonlight. She squeezed her eyes shut causing tears to roll down her cheeks, then buried her face back into her knees.

I sat down beside her and pulled her into a hug. "What's wrong?"

Sobs shook her body. "I-I don't w-w-want to go to first grade," she sputtered.

"Shh," I hushed. I pulled her on to my lap and she relaxed against me as I reclined the patio chair all the way back. "Do you want to see my favorite constellation?"

Kate shifted to lay on her side and rest her head on my shoulder. She took a few shuttering breaths. "W-which one is your favorite?" she asked before sticking her finger in her mouth. Mom had broken her of that habit a year ago, but it still showed up when she was scared. The night had started to cool and I was glad for Kate's body heat as I scanned the sky.

"I don't know if it's dark enough to see it. Do you see those five stars?" I moved my hand in the shape of a "w" pointing to each star in turn.

Kate nodded against my chest.

"That constellation is called Cassiopeia. She was a queen." I pointed to the side of Cassiopeia. "Do you see those four stars? They're really hard to see, but they almost make a lowercase 'n.' That one is called Camelopardalis."

"That's a funny word." Kate laughed. "Camelopardalis," she said, trying it out.

"It means giraffe. A long time ago in ancient Greece, they thought giraffes looked like they had the neck of a camel and the spots of a leopard." I yawned. "So, they put the two words together to make one: camelopard."

"Like Dad does?"

"Yeah," I said.

Kate laughed again. "I like that word," she said, talking over her finger.

"You'll learn a lot of cool stuff in first grade, you know," I said.

"Will I learn about camelopards?"

"You might learn about giraffes. And maybe *you* can teach the rest of your class about camelopards." We sat in silence listening to the crickets and staring at the stars until I had goosebumps on my arms. Kate's breathing had slowed and her sniffing had stopped.

"Are you ready to go to bed?" I asked.

"Do you think Mom will let me sleep in your room?" Kate asked, standing up.

"I think so. I'll ask her. You'll probably need to apologize for earlier, though." I stood and we walked toward the door.

"I know." Kate sighed.

We walked inside and Kate gave Mom a hug and an apology, then climbed the stairs to get ready for bed.

"Thank you so much, *mijita*." Mom pulled me into a tight hug. "I'm glad Kate has a sister like you."

I hugged her back. "Thanks. Is it okay if she sleeps in my room tonight? I know it's a school night but I think she could really use the company."

Mom let me go and held me at arm's length. "*Claro que sí.*" She kissed me on each cheek.

IT TOOK me a long time to fall asleep despite feeling exhausted. My mind wouldn't slow down. I kept thinking of Sidney and Kate and how everything had gone wrong at the party. The scene played over and over in my mind. Carleigh kept telling me to play Spin the Bottle. As I drifted off, I thought of Sidney having cancer at Kate's age, and then having it again and again.

I stood in the same tree house as the dream when I saw Mrs. Black. A breeze blew through the window and rustled the empty hammocks.

A small cough came from across the room. I turned toward the sound looking for the source. Someone lounged in one of the hammocks, reading. They faced away from me so I couldn't see anything more than a few tufts of light brown hair and the book.

I took a step and the floor squeaked underneath my feet. A head poked out from behind the hammock.

"Jessa?" the girl asked. Her voice sounded familiar, but I couldn't place it. Her short spiky hair stuck out from behind a headband.

"Who—" I started.

"It's me, Sidney," she said, cutting me off. "Do you remember me?"

I stared at her for a moment while my brain tried to reconcile the girl in front of me with the little Sidney from the picture in Alexa's room. "Sidney?"

She gave me a big smile.

"This is crazy. I haven't seen you for years," I said, as guilt flooded through me.

It must have shown on my face because Sidney said, "Don't worry about it. A lot of people don't know what to say to a sick kid." Her smile faded and she fidgeted with a beaded bracelet she wore on her wrist. "What are you doing here? Is anything wrong?"

"I don't think so?" My voice rose at the end, making it sound like a question. "I think I'm dreaming. Right?"

Sidney smiled, looking relieved. "Yeah, it's just a dream. C'mon." She walked to the edge of the doorway and instead of turning around and climbing down the ladder, she stepped out into the open air and dropped toward the ground.

"Sidney?" I rushed to the door and looked down expecting to see Sidney sprawled on the forest floor. Why had she jumped off the edge?

I heard a laugh like a bell from above me. I looked up to see Sidney spiraling through the air, swerving through the trees above.

She flipped around and darted back down so she hovered level with the doorway. "What's wrong?"

"I—I thought..." I stammered.

She laughed again with a huge, contagious smile on her face. Instead of feeling stupid, I laughed alongside her.

"Don't worry, you can't get hurt here. That's the whole point of this place." She flew toward me and grabbed my hand, pulling me closer to the edge. "Come fly with me."

"From here?" The idea of jumping out of the tree house made my hands sweat. "I'm going to take the long way down." I turned around and stepped on the first rung of the ladder.

"At least take the fireman's pole," Sidney said, pointing to a long pole I hadn't noticed. "The ladder is broken and sometimes you can get stuck in a loop. Then you never make it to the bottom. You just climb forever." Sidney pointed out two posts sticking out of the pole. "Step on the footholds—it's easier than trying to cling to the pole the whole way down."

I stepped on the posts and wrapped my arms around the pole. It started twisting and I descended in a slow spiral. Sidney flew circles around me until I reached the bottom.

"Let's get you off the ground. I have the perfect place."

Sidney took my hand and led me to a forest path. Her hand felt warm and real.

The hot and humid air caused a trickle of sweat to roll down my back. As Sidney forged ahead through the path, neither of us spoke. I couldn't shake the feeling of reality that accompanied this dream. I couldn't remember a time when I'd been so aware that I *was* dreaming. "Maybe something *is* wrong with me."

"What did you say?" Sidney asked.

Had I said that out loud?

"Are you okay?" Sidney stopped and turned toward me; her eyes squinted in concern.

"No, it's nothing," I said, not wanting Sidney to worry. I shook my head. This was *my* dream; I could tell Dream Sidney anything I wanted to. She wasn't real. "Actually, this place is freaking me out."

Sidney raised her eyebrows. "Why?"

"I'm hyper aware it's a dream, but it feels so real." I started walking and Sidney walked next to me. "Like how I haven't seen you for years but my mind did an incredible job of making you look like a grown-up version of your kindergarten self." I shook my head. "I sound crazy. This is just a dream. You're not real, and I'm in bed."

We walked in silence listening to our footsteps on the forest floor and the song of the birds in the trees. After a few moments, Sidney said in a quiet voice, "I don't think that sounds crazy."

I turned toward her. "Of course, you don't. I made you with my mind." I tapped my forehead for emphasis.

"You didn't."

I stopped and turned to face her. "What are you talking about?"

She closed her eyes and took a slow breath, then opened them. "This isn't *just a dream*. This is real. It's my dream, too."

"What?" I shook my head. "That's crazy."

"It's Dreamland." Sidney had a half smile on her face and her eyes were full of wonder. "It's a place where dreams come true and pain doesn't exist. A safe place for kids who are sick." She looked back at me, concern on her face. "Are *you* sick? Have you been to the hospital recently?"

"No." I took a step back and goosebumps covered my arms. "I mean, I went to the hospital with Mom to get Kate's cast off a few weeks ago. But I'm not sick." Dream Sidney might not be real but she *was* crazy.

"I started coming here right before I was diagnosed with cancer in kindergarten. The other kids here are sick too, though there might be a few who aren't. We're not sure." She floated up off the ground. "This place takes away all the pain. I come here during chemo, anytime I'm feeling sick, or whenever things are too unbearable."

"Wouldn't someone say something? I mean, if it's real, why doesn't the whole world know about it?" My mind spun with ideas. Sidney must be pranking me.

"Ever heard of a fever dream?" She sunk back down to the ground. "That's what most people would call it." She shook her head. "Jessa, I don't know why you're here. I hope you're okay."

"I'm fine." My mind felt like it was going to melt or explode. Like I was thinking of everything and nothing at the same time.

We came to a forked path and stepped into a beam of sunlight. I squinted and Sidney picked the left path.

Neither of us spoke for several minutes. I tried to slow my thoughts down. Could this be real? I pinched myself and it hurt but what did that mean? I'd never understood how or why that worked.

Through the thinning trees, I caught glimpses of the ocean, glittering and sparkling in the sunlight.

"I heard you're sick again," I said to fill the silence while still trying to understand if I spoke to the real Sidney or a dream version. Leaves crunched beneath my feet.

Sidney glanced back at me with a sad smile. "Yeah. This has to be it, though. I don't know how much more I can take." She stopped and turned. One hand fiddled with her beaded bracelet. "After all, third time's the charm, right?"

I crossed my fingers for her. "Right. Third time's the charm."

"Enough with the sick talk. Let's go," Sidney said.

We stepped out of the woods and into an open field on a cliff overlooking the ocean. The hard-packed dirt gave way to a paved area the size of a soccer field.

"What is this?" I tested it with my toes. It wasn't hard like asphalt, but woven and springy.

"It's a trampoline field." She backed up and took a running leap onto the giant tramp, launching herself high into the sky and right over the cliff. I bounced my way to the edge and looked down. Sidney flew low, near the water. A wave crashed and soaked her. She flew back up to me, dripping with salt water and laughing.

She bounced hard and high on the tramp but didn't drop back to the ground like she should have. Instead she floated down, feather slow. Her clothes were dry when she landed next to me.

"That was incredible! You have to teach me."

"It's easy," Sidney said. "Think happy thoughts."

"Seriously?" I shook my head. "That is so cliché."

Sidney laughed. "It works, though." She closed her eyes, rose a few feet off the tramp, and hovered next to me.

"Okay, I'll try it." I closed my eyes, trying to focus on what made me happy. Being popular? I tried to imagine myself with Alexa surrounded by Carleigh, Anna, and the other popular kids going to Sunnyside. They all laughed at something clever I'd said.

I opened my eyes a tiny bit. My feet were still planted on the ground.

"Try again," Sidney called. She flew in a spiral above my head.

I closed my eyes and thought of the time we had checked out a telescope from the library. Jupiter's four biggest moons were in a perfectly straight line, and I had been able to find it so easily. Kate and I had stayed up late that night watching Jupiter move through the sky.

My feet left the tramp and I opened my eyes.

"It worked," I shouted. My feet hovered a foot above the ground. As soon as I realized it, I started to sink. Sidney swooped down and grabbed my hand, trying to pull me up into the sky.

"Keep your happy thoughts alive!" she shouted.

My mind scrambled to find the happy thought. Constellations. Planets. Calming Kate down when she was scared. Family.

Sidney let go. I floundered but stayed floating. "How do I steer?" Panic filled my voice. The waves crashed onto the cliff far below me. With desperation, I clung to the thoughts of my family.

"Lean the way you want to go." Sidney hovered for a minute, then demonstrated.

I stood in the air as though on a high, invisible ladder. The thought of leaning forward terrified me. I didn't want to see the ground far below me.

Sidney hovered over and took both of my hands. "Look at my eyes, don't look down."

I tore my eyes from the water far below and focused them on Sidney's chocolate brown eyes.

"Good. Now lie down on your stomach, like you're in bed."

"I don't like this," I complained. But I let her pull me into a horizontal position. She let go of one hand.

"There you go." She stretched out next to me. "Now, think forward thoughts."

"That doesn't even make sense."

"Try it," Sidney insisted.

I pictured myself moving forward. My body inched forward.

"See? Not too bad." Sidney matched my snail pace. "Now let's go a little faster or we will never be able to get anywhere."

As soon as I thought of flying faster, I did. My hand slid out of Sidney's. "This is unbelievable."

She flew down toward the water, and I followed close behind. My nerves changed to excitement.

I pointed at the cliff. "My dad would love to climb that."

"Why climb when you can fly?" Sidney laughed.

As the sun set, colors reflected off the water painting both the sky and the ocean in yellows, oranges, reds, pinks, and purples. The brightest stars dotted the horizon like glitter.

"Wow."

Sidney sighed next to me. "This is my favorite time of day."

I sighed. "I can see why." I hadn't felt this content for a while. At the same time, I couldn't turn off the one thought running through my head. *Is it real?*

Chapter 4

I awoke in the morning before my alarm. The dream still burned in my mind. *Had Sidney been telling the truth?* I shook my head. Dream Sidney, not real Sidney. In the morning light of my room, the dream seemed to fade. I almost laughed. Why had I worried so much in my dream *about* a dream? It seemed silly now.

Kate was not in her cot. Her blankets were gone. She must have returned to her bed in the middle of the night.

My bed was damp with sweat. After I stripped the sheets, I hopped into the shower.

Today was the first day of school. A pit formed inside me at the thought. At least I had two classes with Alexa.

By the time I dressed, I could hear dishes clanking and my sisters talking downstairs. I heard a soft knock on my door.

"Come in," I called as I ran a brush through my wet hair.

The door opened. "Good, you're up." Mom stepped into my room and glanced at the naked bed. "Bad dream?" she guessed.

"Mom! I didn't pee the bed. I was just really hot last night."

Mom held her hands up in surrender. "I never said you peed the bed, *mijita*."

I rummaged through my shoes and found a pair of cute flats Sarah had thrown out last year because they were "out of style." They'd hardly been worn. I sat down on the bed to put them on.

Mom sat down next to me and squeezed me in a side hug. "Are you excited for school?"

My stomach turned in knots. "It's a whole new school." I tried to ground myself by taking slow breaths but it didn't help.

"It'll be a little different but a lot the same. You'll know a bunch of the kids there, and"—she tucked a stray hair behind my ear—"you'll have Alexa. As long as you have a friend by your side, everything is easier."

When I didn't respond she asked, "What do you want to eat? Sarah wanted cereal, and Kate chose pancakes."

"Breakfast made to order?"

She winked at me through the mirror. "Do you want your traditional omelet?"

"Can I pass?" I tried to smile but it turned out more of a grimace. "Nervous stomach." I couldn't eat a bite of anything.

Mom's eyebrows furrowed and she frowned.

"Pancakes are fine," I amended. I didn't want to make Mom put in any extra work when I wasn't even hungry.

"That's my girl." She squeezed my shoulder one more time. "I'll see you downstairs then."

I blow-dried my hair and took my time getting ready. By the time I made it downstairs, Sarah and Kate had eaten most of their breakfast and I was able to get away with nibbling on half a pancake. My stomach clenched tighter with each swallow.

Sarah tipped up her cereal bowl and drank with a loud slurp.

The sound made me cringe. "That's disgusting," I said.

Sarah gave me a pointed look and took another noisy sip.

"Mom!" I whined.

"Don't slurp your cereal, Sarah," Mom tittered.

Sarah took one last loud slurp, grinning at Mom, then cleared her dish and left to do her hair.

Mom sighed.

I couldn't swallow another bite.

Kate pushed her pancake around on her plate, her face, pale and sticky with syrup.

I reached over and patted Kate's knee. "It's okay to be nervous, but you'll do great." I wiped the syrup off her cheeks. My stomach relaxed a tiny bit and I took a deep breath. Helping Kate always cheered me up.

"But it's all day!" Her teary eyes darted around the room. "What if I don't know anyone in my class? What if I mess up getting my lunch?"

I pulled her into me. "The teachers will help you with lunch. And"—I tickled her sides till she squirmed—"we already know you have the same teacher as your best friend. Everything is easier with a friend by your side. If all else fails, remember the camelopard."

Kate laughed. She shoved another large bite of pancake in her mouth, chewed and swallowed, and gave me a sticky kiss on the cheek.

Mom's mouth curved into a smile.

A few minutes later Mom, Kate, and I piled in the car but Sarah wasn't ready.

"What is she doing in there?" I glanced at the clock, regretting the half pancake I'd eaten. "We're going to be late. On the first day."

Mom sighed and honked the horn.

Sarah took her sweet time. I couldn't keep my eyes off the clock as I counted off the seconds in my mind. After three minutes Mom went inside to find her. Seven minutes in, Mom came back out, muttering in Spanish under her breath. Ten full minutes after we had climbed into the car, Sarah finally came out. She'd done a delicate lace braid that wrapped around one side of her head and ended in a soft bun.

"Wow," Kate said. "You look like you're getting married or something."

Sarah beamed.

"It took you long enough," I grumbled. The knots in my stomach tightened. "Can you drop me off first?" I begged.

"The high school is first on the way," Mom said.

"But Sarah made us all late!" I protested. Typical Sarah. "And now she's going to be the only one on time."

Sarah turned from the front passenger seat and gave me a smug smile.

"Sorry, Jessa. This is the way that makes most sense," Mom said. She dropped Sarah off at the high school first. Kate gave me a panicked look as we approached the middle school.

I reached over and squeezed her hand. "You're going to rock it."

The second bell rang as I got out of the car. *Great. I'm late on my first day.*

With any luck, Alexa had saved me a seat.

I navigated through the empty halls to Mr. Black's class. When I walked in, Mr. Black stood at the front of the room by the whiteboard reading the roll.

He looked up. "Ah, Miss Newberry. Did you get a tardy slip from the office?"

The whole class turned toward me and I froze in place.

A couple of kids giggled.

I noticed Alexa sitting in the back of the room. She wore cute, designer skinny jeans with artful rips and holes in them. I groaned. Why did I have to shop at the thrift store? At least my shirt was new, sort of.

"I'll let it slide today but, in the future"—he raised his voice and spoke to the whole class—"if you are late, you'll need to get a tardy slip from the office or I can't let you into class."

He turned back to me. "Find a seat, please." Then he focused his attention on roll call.

I wiped my sweaty hands on my jeans—why did all of my

pants have holes in the knees?—and looked around with rising anxiety.

Carleigh and Anna sat next to each other on the back row with Alexa right in front of Carleigh. Alexa made eye contact with me and mouthed, "Sorry," as she pointed to the seat across from her. Then she shrugged. Instead of the empty seat I'd hoped for, one of the boys from the party sat across from Alexa. He kept glancing back toward Carleigh.

The last empty seat in the room sat front and center. I couldn't believe Alexa hadn't saved me a seat near her. Mr. Black started writing the class rules on the whiteboard. My shoes felt like they were filled with lead.

I could feel every eye on me as I walked across the room and up one of the rows. I tripped on something—probably my own feet—and landed on the floor. A few people laughed.

Scrambling to my feet, I slunk into my chair and tried to become invisible. My ears were burning as Mr. Black called the class to order and started going over the rules. I stared straight at the red ink on the whiteboard but didn't take in any words.

When I could feel the blush leave my face, I chanced a look at the kids next to me. On my left, a girl I didn't know with red braids and pale, freckled skin was furiously taking notes. I glanced to my right. Michael sat at the desk next to me. He gave me a small smile I couldn't return.

"Please stand up and introduce yourselves to the class, starting here." Mr. Black pointed to the front corner desk two down from me. "State your first and last name, which school you're coming from, and something you like to do or a hobby you have."

The girl sitting in the corner stood and started speaking. I didn't hear any of it. My mind started whirling. I didn't know what to say. Did I have a hobby? What if I said something stupid?

Red Braids stood up next.

My fingers felt numb.

My brain hyper focused, bringing random details to my attention. Mr. Black's cluttered desk had everything from papers to a golden padlock with a picture on it. Was that the Eiffel Tower? Why was his desk so messy on the first day?

The carpet in front of me had several circular stains on it.

Red Braids—had she said her name was Claire?—finished talking and sat down.

My turn.

What was my name again? What were my hobbies?

I stood and turned to face the class. Everyone stared at me. My stomach churned as though I'd eaten gravel for breakfast.

"Um... My name is..." My mind went completely blank.

"Louder!" a boy from the back of the room called. A few kids giggled.

Heat filled my cheeks and a lump grew in my throat.

In a panic now, I tried again. "My name is..."

Someone else laughed. I could hear whispering.

Mr. Black stepped up next to me and put his hand on my shoulder. "Jessa?"

"My name is Jessa!" I shouted with triumph. The whispers changed to laughter. My eyes stung.

No. I couldn't cry now.

I swallowed hard, determined to finish. "I went to Meadow Brook," I heard myself say. My mouth had taken over. "And I like puzzles."

The class erupted with laughter.

Why had I said that? I did like puzzles, but only with Kate or my *abuela*.

"I like puzzles too," Mr. Black said. I wanted to die. He had just made everything worse. Nobody wanted to like the same thing as their teacher.

"You can sit down now," Mr. Black said.

I plopped down and put my head on my desk, trying to hide. I had totally ruined my chances of making a good impression. I would be the puzzle girl for the rest of my school life.

I kept my head on my desk and didn't listen to anyone else's introduction. I didn't look up when Mr. Black assigned lockers or when he handed out textbooks. My face felt sunburned. I kept it hidden until the bell rang and the class had exited the room. Finally, I followed. I needed Alexa.

I pushed through the crowded hallway to my locker. Momentary relief came when I saw Alexa standing near it but disappeared when I realized she was talking to Carleigh and Anna.

Carleigh looked up first, then nudged Alexa who extracted herself from the other girls and walked over to me. Alexa wrapped me up in a hug. "I tried to save you a seat but that boy, Drew, took it. Why were you late? What happened?" She squeezed me a little tighter. "And why did you say you liked doing puzzles of all things? Everyone is saying you like doing puzzles *with* Mr. Black."

I couldn't open my mouth to speak because my tears would come before my first word. I pulled away from Alexa and covered my face.

"It's not that bad," she said, trying to be nice.

I took a deep breath. "Yes, it is." I dropped my hands away from my face. "Nobody will want to be friends with me now." I found myself looking over at Carleigh as she laughed with Anna. Her light blue shirt had something French scrawled across it in cursive. She wore a scarf around her neck to complete the look of not caring but still looking trendy. I tugged on my new shirt from the discount store.

Carleigh looked up and caught me staring. She said something to the ring of girls around her locker, who all laughed

—a few glanced over at me. Anna whispered something else and flipped her long hair.

I was supposed to be *in* the ring of popular girls, not being laughed at by them. "I don't know what to do," I moaned.

Alexa grabbed my hand. "I'll take care of this for you. I'll do damage control. No one will even remember this next week."

"Really?" I asked.

"Really," Alexa replied.

The bell rang and we headed to our classes. I could make it through the day knowing Alexa was on my side.

FOR THE REST of the week, I hid in the library during lunch break and ate alone.

Alexa hadn't talked to me much at school since the first day. She'd sat with Carleigh, Anna, and the other girls who'd laughed at me in class and spent the whole lunch break with them.

Damage control. Right?

On Thursday, I smiled at Carleigh. She smirked back at me and whispered something to Anna. They both looked at me and giggled.

My face burned.

Mr. Black had not turned out to be the teacher Sarah described. He roamed the halls during his free period and lunch, yelling at anyone he caught in the halls. He caught me once on my way back to class from the bathroom. I had a hall pass, but he wouldn't accept it. He followed me back to science to make sure I didn't skip. When I told Mom about it, she said he missed Mrs. Black and to not take it personally.

By the time Friday came, I couldn't help but celebrate the start of Labor Day weekend. I needed an extra day off school.

I tossed my backpack on the couch when I got home, bypassed Mom in the kitchen, and headed straight upstairs to my room. I could smell fresh-baked cookies, but instead of enticing me they made my stomach turn.

Once in the safety of my room I flopped onto my bed. My pillow felt extra soft and cool to my warm skin. The fan blew a gentle breeze over me. My heavy eyelids drooped and my head ached. I could close my eyes for a minute, right?

When I opened them, the tree house surrounded me. All of the worries from school melted away. I looked for Sidney, but I didn't see her. We'd had so much fun last time. Could I fly without her? I wanted to try.

I closed my eyes and thought of the way Kate crawled in bed with me when she had a bad dream. When she'd wanted *me* on her first roller coaster ride instead of Mom or Dad. How she'd broken her arm over the summer, and I was able help her stay calm so she wouldn't have to be sedated.

My feet lifted off the ground. My eyes shot open. I *could* do this alone.

I flew through the door and out into the open air. The wind rushed past me as I climbed. I felt so free. For the first time in a week I could be myself. I laughed as I swooped up and down like a roller coaster. I flew higher and higher until the island looked like a green and brown puddle. The view took my breath away.

The forest took up most of one side. A stream ran through it turning into a powerful waterfall and dumping into a bright blue lagoon. A giant mountain sat in the middle, dividing the island in half. On the far side, white sand beaches sprawled beneath palm trees.

I dove straight back down toward the trees and hovered above the top of the mountain. The sun stood high in the sky and the light flashed off the rolling waves.

I dropped down so close to the river I could have reached my hand out and touched it as I flew. The river led me through the forest to a grove of trees. As I flew, a roaring sound grew louder and louder until I came to the edge of the land. The thunderous sound of water pounding over rocks engulfed me. Within seconds I'd flown over the waterfall. I followed it down to the lagoon, flying parallel with it, as though I planned to dive into the water. For fun, I did a flip, like the divers I'd seen in the Olympics. Mist engulfed me. I finished my flip but was disoriented. Which way was up? Attempting to get out of the mist, I flew the way I thought the horizon would be. Instead I almost ran into the rocky cliff.

Jerking to a halt before I ran into the cliff, I switched directions and flew upward, but my hand splashed into the lagoon. Before I realized it, the force of the waterfall pushed me all the way under.

The current from the waterfall caught me and tossed me about. The seconds felt like hours. Water rushed up my nose and any air I'd been holding was forced out of me.

A hand grabbed mine and pulled. I didn't resist. My rescuer pulled me up and up until my face broke the water and onto the beach nearby. I coughed, gasping for breath. When I opened my eyes, I saw my rescuer—a girl, about my age. Her sandy-blonde hair streaked with bright pink and aquamarine was pulled into hundreds of tiny braids.

Concern filled her ocean blue eyes. "Are you okay?" she asked. "I got to you as soon as I could."

"Y-yes," I stuttered. I took a deep breath, hoping to slow my racing heart.

"You ought to be more careful around the waterfall." She let go of my hand and swam away.

"Wait! Who are you?" I yelled.

Instead of answering she dove down into the water. A

shimmering aquamarine tail flipped up into the air then disappeared.

A mermaid?

"Jessa!" Sarah called from downstairs.

The world shifted around me. "Get your butt down here!"

I opened my eyes. My clothes were drenched in sweat. "Coming!" I shouted back. The breeze from my fan made me shiver. I changed my clothes and left the damp covers for later.

Downstairs, Mom set out dishes for spaghetti and meatballs with mint lemonade. Kate smiled when I came in and patted the seat next to her. I obliged and sat.

"Why is your hair all sweaty?" Sarah asked.

"I fell asleep and had a bad dream," I told her.

"Don't forget about the fun run for Sidney Thatcher tomorrow," Mom reminded us.

"Do I have to?" Sarah said, tucking in a loose strand of hair that fallen from her messy bun.

"We support our friends and neighbors. We're doing it," Dad said firmly.

"I think it sounds fun," I said.

Sarah rolled her eyes and shoved a bobby pin back into her bun.

"I picked and washed the mint leaves for the lemonade," Kate bragged. I could tell. She'd gotten a few bits of stem along with the leaves.

"Nice job, sis." I held up my hand for a fist bump and we both made the explosion noise at the same time. The normalcy comforted me after my dream.

"If it's minty lemonade, could we call it mlemonade or mintonade?" Dad asked, a little twinkle in his eyes.

Mom laughed from the other side of the room.

I rolled my eyes. "Those are both awful."

"I like mintonade," Kate said. She almost always gave it to him.

Sarah scrunched her nose. "I'm with Jessa—they both suck." She dished a pile of spaghetti onto her plate. "Mlemonade? Really Dad? You're better than that."

"Honey, we have two for and two against," he said to Mom. "You're the tie breaker."

"That's a lot of pressure." Mom wiped her hands on a towel and joined us at the table. "I'm going to have to side with Sarah and Jessa, though. Neither of them works."

Dad clutched his chest as though he'd been shot by an arrow and we all laughed.

Chapter 5

A crowd filled the high school football field. Hundreds of people had come out to support Sidney's fun run. A few people ran warmup laps around the track.

Mom handed out our numbers and we took turns pinning them on each other. As soon as Mom pinned Sarah's number on her back, Sarah disappeared into her group of friends.

"Is a fun run called a frun?" Dad asked as he put the number on my back.

"I could give it to you." I smiled.

"That's almost too easy." He reached over, tugging on a few strands of hair on the top of my head.

"Dad!" I touched my hair feeling loops of hair sticking straight up instead of slicked back into my ponytail like they were supposed to be.

"It's a shark fin!" He laughed.

"You're way too pleased with yourself." I redid my ponytail, all the while glaring playfully at him.

Kate slipped her hand into mine once I'd fixed my hair. "Can you run with me?"

"No problem." I squeezed her hand then called to Mom, "I've got Kate."

"*Gracias, chiquita,*" she said with a nod. Dad slipped his hand into hers, and they kissed. They were so embarrassing.

In the middle of the field an announcer sat at a table with a microphone. "Ladies and gentlemen, thank you for coming to the fun run for Sidney Thatcher. We've raised almost five thousand dollars. The Thatcher family thanks you for your generous donations to help pay for her treatments. Over a hundred people have signed up for the race today, which will begin in ten minutes."

"C'mon, Kate. Let's stretch." As I led her to the field I looked around for Sidney. Was she here or was she too sick? Would she look like the sick girl in the posters from years ago or more like she did in my dreams? What if we ran into each other? Was she also really having the same dreams?

Kate and I reached the field and we both sat down. Kate copied me as I methodically stretched the different muscle groups in my legs like I'd learned in gym.

"Now you do my stretches," Kate said, still lying on the ground. She stretched and sat up like she'd just woken up. I copied her. She climbed to her feet and I followed. She rolled her shoulders back, and stuck her chest out.

When I laughed, she turned toward me. "You *have* to do it, Jessa."

I complied. With each roll something on my left side near my collarbone popped. What was that?

"Runners, take your places!" the announcer called, pulling my attention away from the popping.

I herded Kate over to the lineup.

Anna, from school, stood in the middle of the crowd with her long hair in a ponytail. I smiled at her. She cocked an eyebrow and pushed her way closer to the starting line next to— Alexa! I wanted to call out, but the crowd shifted and I couldn't see her anymore.

Did they come together?

"Three..." the announcer called.

Was this still "damage control"?

"Two..."

Kate squeezed my hand. I pushed the girls at school out of my mind. Today wasn't about them.

"One..."

BANG!

The crowd surged forward. I held Kate's hand tight. I didn't want to lose her or let her get trampled by the anxious crowd. Some people took these things too seriously. They didn't understand the *fun* part of the fun run. Kate and I were not those people.

We jogged through the 5k course—walking whenever we got tired. At the first water station, Kate took a big drink, turned toward me, and spat it out in a perfect stream, soaking my shirt.

"Kate!" I shrieked.

She laughed and ran from me.

I couldn't help but laugh as I chased her down. I caught up to her at the next water booth. I grabbed a cup, took a big mouthful, and spat some on her.

The lady at the water booth frowned.

We kept going. At the next water stand, Kate started spitting water on me again. Instead of spitting back, I dumped the whole cup on her head. She squealed and ran away.

Each stand that we passed after that, we grabbed a few cups of water. One for drinking and the rest for the water fight we'd started.

By the time we crossed the finish line, we both looked like we'd fallen into a pool.

When we met back up with Mom and Dad, they laughed at us.

Kate pulled my arm and I leaned down. "Let's get 'em," she whispered.

Kate filled her mouth and turned toward Dad. He pulled Mom in front of him just before a fountain of water sprang from Kate's mouth. Mom got soaked.

Kate laughed. She and Mom, both big cheeked from mouthfuls of water, chased Dad as he ran away.

"Jessa?" a voice from behind me called.

I turned and saw a girl sitting in a chair under an umbrella. Sidney? All of her hair was gone, even her eyebrows and lashes. Her pale skin looked almost translucent. The medical mask she wore covered up her mouth and nose.

I bit my lip. "Hi." She seemed familiar but also like a stranger. "Sorry you have cancer again." Why did I say that? I wanted to hide in the awkward silence that followed.

Sidney raised her bare eyebrows.

I kept talking—filling the silence—hoping I wouldn't put my foot back in my mouth.

"I hope you beat it this time. I mean, third time's the charm, right?" I felt a little déjà vu as I repeated the same line she'd said in my dream.

Sidney tilted her head, a small smile played in her eyes. "Do you like *Peter Pan*, or is it too cliché?"

My eyes grew wide. "What did you say?" I looked around. We were alone but I still leaned in. "No way."

The gleam in Sidney's eyes looked triumphant. "You believe me now?"

"What are you talking about?" I asked, still in denial that we'd shared a dream.

"Dreamland." She grabbed my arm and squeezed it lightly. "It's okay. For years I thought it was just a dream too."

"Seriously?" *Could this be true?*

"But you were there too, I *know* it."

I shook my head again. "Sidney, you're saying we shared a dream. That's impossible."

"C'mon, Jessa, don't play dumb. We were there together. We both know it." She pulled softly on my arm and I bent down close enough that my ear almost touched her mask. "You have to meet me there again."

I pulled back and looked into her eyes.

"Jessa!" Alexa's voice rang through the field.

"I've gotta go." I nodded in Alexa's direction.

"There's a cave behind the waterfall where we all meet. Go there next time," Sidney whispered. Her pleading eyes softened my resolve.

"Jessa!" Alexa called again. I could see her walking towards us.

"Please?" Sidney asked. "If it's not real, then it's not going to matter, right?"

"Okay," I said.

Sidney released my arm and I trotted toward Alexa.

"Where have you been, and why are you soaking wet?" Alexa asked, putting her arm through mine. "Did you run? I ended up running with Anna. My mom wanted to meet her, and this was the easiest way. Sorry I didn't invite you."

"How's it going with Carleigh?" My chest loosened. Alexa and I were still best friends. She had run with Anna because Mrs. Johnston wanted to meet Anna. That made sense.

"Oh my gosh, I found out Drew likes Carleigh!" Alexa blurted out.

"Who's Drew?" I asked.

Alexa launched into a long explanation about Drew, the "captain of the soccer team and the cutest boy on it" and why he and Carleigh would make the perfect couple.

I wanted to ask how the damage control was going, but I couldn't get a word in. Alexa would tell me about it when she was ready and not a moment before.

Instead I thought of what Sidney had said. Could it really be real?

I DIDN'T HAVE another dream for five days. Each morning I woke up disappointed that I hadn't gone. I wanted to try flying again. And I couldn't get what Sidney had said out of my head.

After a few more days of being teased by my class and ignored by Alexa, I went to bed and woke up in Dreamland.

I was alone in the tree house. Deep inside I felt Sidney was right about this place. I'd heard of recurring dreams, but this seemed different. I felt in total control. It didn't feel like a regular dream. But right now, it didn't matter. I was here and I wanted to have fun.

What was my happy thought? Maybe last year when Mom let Alexa come with us to the planetarium.

I hovered above the floor, making sure I could fly before jumping out of the doorway. I let myself free fall most of the way, then pulled up and rose above the treetops.

The whole island sprawled out before me. The lagoon and waterfall were off to my right. Mermaids lay on rocks, sunning themselves.

Real mermaids. Well, maybe not *actually* real.

I flew towards the mermaids. I wanted to get a closer look at them—maybe find the one who rescued me and thank her.

The air whipped past me as I sped above the trees. I swooped down close to the river. I shot out above the waterfall and took one lazy loop before looking for my mermaid rescuer.

Below, in the cove, about twenty mermaids and mermen lay on large rocks or sandy beaches. Their tails—all various shades of blue and green—shimmered in the sunlight. Each one had a base of blonde or brown hair with chunky streaks of a few bright colors that matched their tails.

There. I spotted the mermaid with pink and aquamarine

streaks in her hair and an aquamarine tail. She had saved me; I was sure of it. I flew down toward the lagoon.

"Jessa, you came!" I heard from behind me.

I turned around. Sidney hovered in front of the waterfall. Though she should have been wet from the mist and the water, her hair and clothes were dry.

"Hey, Sidney." I turned my head to see the mermaids again, but they'd all dived into the water.

Sidney gave a wide smile. "Do you like the mermaids?"

"Their tails are so pretty," I said. "And their hair is pretty cool, too. I like how it matches." I turned back toward Sidney. "Where'd they go?"

"Well, they're pretty shy. They're here because of Lauren."

"Who's Lauren?"

"She's a friend of mine. This place has a lot of kids in it. Each time a new kid comes, something changes here. I think Dreamland gives each kid what they need most to help them cope with their illness. When Lauren was here the first time, Dreamland gave her mermaids." Sidney waved me closer. "She's inside. Do you want to meet her?"

I nodded. "What'd Dreamland give you?"

Sidney gave a hesitant smile. "It's a bit of a journey to get there. Maybe another time?"

"Okay."

"C'mon. There's so much I want to show you." Sidney took my hand and started pulling me toward the waterfall.

"Wait, I don't want to go near the waterfall. Last time it pulled me down."

"I'll help you," Sidney promised. "I've done this hundreds of times." She gave a gentle tug on my hand and I let her tow me toward the raging water. "Hold your breath. You don't have to, but I think it helps."

I took a deep breath and held it. She squeezed my hand and

I squeezed hers back. My stomach fluttered, but it didn't feel clenched and tight like in the real world.

I plugged my nose and closed my eyes. Before I could chicken out, Sidney flew through and pulled me with her. The deafening water pounded on my head and shoulders, filling my ears.

Was I sinking?

My hand started to slip out of Sidney's. I wanted to stop and go back, but Sidney gave me one more tug. The pressure of the water disappeared, and we popped out the back side by the rocky cliff.

I opened my eyes. I was floating behind the fall. We made it.

Relief flooded through me and I let out a whoop of excitement that the pounding of the waterfall drowned out. Sidney laughed—or at least it looked like she laughed.

She flew up and into a small, dark opening. I could see no path leading to it. Was this only accessible by flying? Maybe someone could climb the rock if they were careful.

I let myself rise until I was level with the entrance, then flew forward until my feet hit the stone.

The damp ground chilled my bare feet, making me shiver as I walked into the cave. The musty smell of earth engulfed me. Rough, stone walls with stalactites and stalagmites jutting off the floors and ceilings helped form a natural path for us to follow. The tips of some of the stalagmites glowed dimly and lit the way. Echoes of laughter came from ahead.

The thought of meeting kids I didn't know brought flashbacks of my first day of school and filled me with nerves.

"C'mon," Sidney said, as though she'd sensed my reluctance, "they're nice."

I took a slow breath and followed Sidney forward. A brightness shone from somewhere in front of us. What if the new kids didn't want me here? I thought of the girls at school. I couldn't handle anymore drama right now.

The light grew brighter. Little crystals in the walls and ceiling sparkled and flashed around us. The passage became wider.

A group of kids sat on logs around a small fire. Behind them dozens of hammocks, similar to the ones in the tree house, hung haphazardly along the walls. A few were occupied with kids reading or playing hand-held video games. The rest of the kids crowded around a table engrossed in a game of Dungeons and Dragons.

The air tasted stale and a bit damp. My clothes dripped onto the earthen floor. I glanced over at Sidney—she was as dry as she'd been outside. *How had she done that?*

A boy about our age sitting on a stump by the fire looked up at us. "Hey, Sid." He stood and smiled at both of us. "Who's your friend?" The other kids stopped what they were doing and looked up.

"Rafa, this is Jessa." She gestured toward the boy. "Jessa, this is Rafa."

Rafa gave me a half wave. "Any friend of Sidney's is a friend of mine."

"Likewise, I guess." I said with an awkward wave back.

"Jessa's new here," Sidney said.

"Welcome," Rafa said as he made his way over to us. "Whatcha in for?"

I looked at Sidney, not sure how to respond.

She gave me a reassuring smile. "He's asking if you know why you're here."

"Sidney!" A boy playing Dungeons and Dragons waved to her. She waved back and started walking over.

"Oh, right." My face burned but I cleared my throat and

focused on Rafa, determined to make a good impression. "I'm not sure why."

"I hear ya." Rafa clapped me on the shoulder. A strand of dark brown hair fell into his face and he tucked it behind his ear. "I'm still not sure why I'm here."

"I'm still betting on a coma," the boy who'd waved to Sidney called out.

Rafa rolled his eyes and walked over toward Sidney and his friends. I let out a sigh. I hadn't made a total fool of myself. Why couldn't I do that at school?

As Sidney and Rafa talked, I studied him. Up close, I could tell he was a few years older than me. He had an unusual patchwork of clothes, like he'd sewn several brown and green shirts together to make one. On anyone else it would have looked bad, but on him it looked great.

I looked down at my clothes—Sarah's hand-me-downs, but now soaking wet. How were their clothes dry? Sidney walked back over to me, giving the boys at the table a wave, and Rafa followed her.

"What is this place? A hideout?" I asked. The cave was bigger than I could see from where I stood. Several tunnels branched off, leading deeper underground.

Sidney gave a chuckle and started down one of the tunnels. "Kind of."

Rafa gave me a half grin. "Legend says a long time ago, this all used to be in the tree house but as more kids came, more things showed up to entertain them. Eventually the tree house was over loaded, so they moved down here."

We emerged into another room. "This is the library—clearly not the most popular place."

A small bookshelf with a few books on it sat against one wall. Beanbags and soft chairs were scattered throughout. A few people were sprawled across them, reading. Small, translucent stones, set into the wall, gave off a soft light, perfect for reading.

"Where are all the books?" I asked.

Sidney grabbed a book off the shelf and handed it to me. "It turns into whatever you want to read. Try it."

I took the book and opened it to the middle. I recognized it as *Harry Potter and the Goblet of Fire*. "This is what I'm reading at home." I looked a little closer. "Cool. It opened to the same spot." I read a few sentences.

A blonde girl about my age stood up and walked over to us. The pink and purple streaks in her hair reminded me of the mermaids. "It's *my* favorite place," she said with a smile at Rafa.

Rafa smiled back. "I prefer the game room. I'm not the most avid reader." He winked at her.

"Are you new?" she asked me but didn't wait for me to respond. "I'm Lauren." Her arm was around Rafa's waist.

"Jessa," I said, trying not to gawk. They seemed so cool.

"Nice to meet you, Jessa." Lauren smiled then turned to Rafa. "You didn't even dry her off?"

Rafa shrugged, but Lauren closed her eyes and placed her hand on my shoulder. Heat surged through my clothes and dried them. Lauren opened her eyes and dropped her hand down to her side. "Sorry, we're still working on his manners."

Rafa gave her a playful push.

"Do you know why you're here?" Lauren asked.

"I think it's another fluke, like Rafa," Sidney said.

"This is my second time here," Lauren said. "The first time I came I was like seven and I had been burned really bad—like eighty-five percent of my body."

"Wow," I said, and Rafa nodded sympathetically.

"I was in the hospital for a long time. When I got better, I stopped having these dreams," Lauren said. "A few months ago, I was in a serious car accident. I've been in the hospital since."

"I'm sorry," I said, not sure what else to say.

"Thanks." Lauren shrugged. "I love this place. I don't love the problems I'm having, but at least I'm among friends."

Sidney nodded. "I started coming here right before they diagnosed me with cancer the first time. When I had finished my treatments, the dreams stopped coming—until I relapsed. That was actually how I knew my cancer was back this time."

"But I still don't know why I'm here," Rafa said. "I've been here for as long as I can remember, and I never leave. I was here before Lauren and Sidney came their first times."

"Do you think there is something wrong with me?" I asked. "I mean, I do leave. I wake up and go to school and stuff."

"I've seen a lot of kids show up a couple of times and then never again," Rafa said. "If you're not sick, you'll stop coming. Sometimes people stumble into this place and stumble out of it later."

Lauren nodded then reached out and touched my shoulder. "Don't worry about it, Jessa. I'm sure you're fine." She went back to her bean bag and book.

"Let me show you the rest of the place," Rafa said.

"Come on." Sidney took my hand and we followed Rafa down another tunnel.

What if they're right and I am sick? I didn't feel sick—that almost made things worse. *Could all this be real?*

"Lauren is the girl I told you about." Sidney broke into my thoughts.

"What?" I asked.

"You know, who the mermaids are here for. She doesn't like to talk about it," Sidney whispered as we followed. "Like she said, she was seven the first time she came, so Dreamland gave her the mermaids. The mermaids love her. They copy her style —that's why they've got color in their hair like hers." Sidney chuckled. "She's changed the color so many times, and the mermaids always mimic her. They can even change the color of their tails. One time she went total goth with black hair and black nail polish and lipstick and stuff. The mermaids looked like they'd emerged from a black-and-white movie. She says it drives her crazy, though, she loves swimming and playing water polo with them, so I don't think she minds too much." Sidney laughed and I laughed along with her. I felt so relaxed around her.

We reached a doorway. Rafa stepped back and let us go first. Jammed with kids, a room the size of our school gym was full of all kinds of games. Old arcade games lined one wall—the big bulky kind Dad played as a kid, including Pac-Man, Space Invaders, Frogger, and Q-Bert. At the end of a room several huge TVs hung on the walls with video games in progress. Kids crowded around the players, laughing and talking. The middle of the room was full of games that needed a big table, like pool, foosball, air hockey, and ping pong. A few dart boards hung on a wall near us.

My jaw dropped. "What is this place?"

"The Rec Room," Rafa said. I could hear the smile in his voice.

"How does it all work?" I asked in amazement.

"Magic?" Sidney guessed. "Who cares? This place is epic."

"Wait till you see the arboretum." Rafa smiled.

"The arbo what?" I asked.

"Rafa!" a boy called from the crowd of gamers gathered around the TVs.

Rafa waved at him then raised his eyebrows and nodded toward the TVs. "Duty calls."

Sidney linked her arm through mine and pulled me away from the Rec Room.

"Everyone seems nice," I said as we walked out.

"Yeah, they're great." Sidney led me down another tunnel.

"What's an arbor—whatever?" I asked as the noise died down.

"An arboretum?" Sidney corrected. "I'll show you."

She stopped at the entrance to a new room and let me enter first. A forest surrounded me though we were still in a room in the cave.

The sheer walls shot straight up and sunlight spilled through a large hole in the high ceiling. Plants covered the ground around the colorful trees and flowers bloomed everywhere.

Sidney came and stood next to me and sighed. "Isn't it great?"

I didn't respond right away. Yeah, it was pretty, but no different from the beauty of the whole island.

"Um..." I stalled. "How is this better than the Rec Room?"

"I thought the same thing when I first saw it. Close your eyes." She commanded.

I closed my eyes and let Sidney lead me into the trees.

"Notice the smells while we're walking."

With each step I smelled something new. First flowery smells like roses and lavender, then herbal smells like rosemary and oregano, then... "It smells like pizza," I said, my stomach growling.

Sidney laughed. "Open your eyes."

I did. We were walking right next to a row of bushes with bite-sized pizza bagels hanging off them like ornaments. "What the..." I trailed off. Sidney picked one and popped it in her mouth. I grabbed one too. The melted cheese stuck to my fingers, burning. "Ouch! They're hot!" I sucked my finger for a moment.

"They're tasty," Sidney said, picking out another one.

Steam rose off the hot cheese, but I took a bite anyway. I tasted the perfect ratio of bagel, cheese, sauce, and meat in each bite. "Holy cow, these taste better than anything in real life." I popped the whole thing in my mouth and carefully chewed. It burned my tongue, but I couldn't stop myself; I picked two more and ate as we walked.

As we entered a grove of trees, the smells turned from savory to sweet, like we'd stepped into an ice cream or candy shop.

Sidney didn't stop until we were surrounded by trees, but not just any trees. Bright red, brown, orange, and yellow leaves covered some of them. Other trees had neon green, hot pink, or purple leaves. All were dotted with flowers and fruit. It looked like autumn and spring had combined into something so much better.

"Wow," I exhaled. The air temperature had dropped, and I could now see my breath.

"You've got to try these." Sidney plucked a piece of fruit from the branch of the blue-leafed tree next to her and took a bite.

I picked a pale pink fruit about the size and shape of an apple but soft like a ripe plum, and cold, like it had just come out of the fridge.

Sidney's was more of a pear shape. She took another bite. "Mmm, this one is my favorite."

"What is it?" I asked. I squeezed it softly.

"Delicious." Sidney took another bite, a little bit of brown juice dribbled down her chin and she wiped it clean with her hand.

I bit into the fruit. The cold and creamy inside cooled my mouth down after the pizza bagels. "Is this strawberry ice cream?" I asked. I took another bite and looked at Sidney with wide eyes.

"The ice cream trees are my favorite. There are tons of different flavors. And over here"—she walked over to a small garden—"we have a candy garden." She picked a fruit from a vine on the ground and handed me a tiny watermelon. Sidney picked another one for her and broke it open with her fingernails. I imitated her, digging my fingernails into the waxy skin of the tiny melon. Inside were tiny slices of sour watermelon candy. I pulled out a few and ate them. The flavor exploded over my tongue. First the sweet of the sugared outside then so sour I made a face, followed by just enough sweet that I wanted to eat another.

"This is way better than what you can buy at the store!" I exclaimed.

"All the plants in here are edible, and they're all delicious. We have gumball pebbles. The bark on all the trees are different types of crackers. The grass is licorice and the rocks are made of taffy. And when you get tired of candy and junk, you can go over to the far end," Sidney pointed at the wall farthest from where we entered, "and find real fruits and vegetables always in season and ready to eat."

I smiled at Sidney. "This is incredible."

"I know." Sidney smiled back. "Do you believe me?"

I shrugged. "I want to, but I'm afraid of what it means for me. Am I sick too?"

"Maybe, maybe not." Sidney put her arm around me. "But if you are, I'll be there for you."

"Thanks," I said. Her words and gesture didn't change anything, but I felt better.

After Sidney and I sampled as much of the candy-fruit we could handle, we went back to the Rec Room. Lauren and Rafa challenged us to a game of foosball, where they won spectacularly thanks to my abysmal goalkeeping. We played video games for the rest of the night.

Why had I been worried about meeting up with Sidney?

Chapter 6

I awoke before my alarm the next morning and lay in bed, enjoying the breeze of the fan on my face. I felt lighter and happier than I had in a long time.

My alarm went off and I forced myself out of bed and headed to the shower. I couldn't wait to get back to Dreamland. I'd never had a dream like that. And, if I believed Sidney, maybe it wasn't a dream; maybe it was real.

I got ready and headed downstairs. Kate sat at the bar in the kitchen eating breakfast while Mom styled her hair. I slumped onto the stool next to Kate and grabbed a pancake. I already felt full. Did the dream food fill you up in real life?

"Sit up, Jessa," Mom said.

I rolled my shoulders back, and the thing around my collarbone popped in and out. I had forgotten about it. "Mom, there's something by my collarbone. It pops in and out when I roll my shoulders."

Mom paused Kate's hairstyle—one hand holding the half-finished braid and a bobby pin sticking out from between her lips. "Let me see."

I pulled down the collar of my shirt so she could see my collarbone. I rolled my shoulder. Pop. Pop.

"Huh." Mom put her spare hand on the spot where it popped. "Do it again."

I did. Pop. Pop. Pop.

"That's weird." She pressed on it. "Does it hurt?"

"No. It's annoying, though." I dumped jam on my pancake and cut it into little pieces, never taking a bite.

"John, come feel this," Mom said to Dad as he came down the stairs. She made me roll my shoulders again.

"That's different. It feels like a little lump," Dad said. He walked over to the couch, sat down, and turned on the news.

Mom turned her attention back to Kate's hair, but she had a far-off look in her eyes as she worked.

Sarah came downstairs, eyes on her phone. She grabbed a piece of toast and almost missed her mouth.

"Sarah, no phones during meals," Mom reminded.

"Sorry, Mom, but the latest hair tutorial just dropped and I want to figure it out."

"Shh," Dad said, tying his shoes while trying to catch the weather report.

"You know you can look that up on your phone, right?" Sarah asked, holding up her phone.

Dad threw a pillow at Sarah, which caused Mom to say, "John!" in an appalled tone and toss the pillow back to the couch. She turned back to Sarah and held out her hand. "Phone."

Sarah rolled her eyes. But she slapped her phone into Mom's outstretched hand.

I tuned out their ever-going argument and focused on the TV as I ate my breakfast. The weather report ended and a picture flashed of a little boy Kate's age. The caption under the picture read *Six-year-old drowns in neighbor's pool.*

"Jessa," Mom said. I looked over at her. She'd finished Kate's hair. "Focus on your food, please. We're going to be late." As if to prove her point, an alarm on her phone rang, reminding us that we needed to get in the car within the next five minutes to get to school on time.

Dad shut the TV off and gave Mom a kiss before he headed out the door.

We piled into the car and dropped Sarah off first.

"I'll see you after school," Mom said when she dropped me off next.

"Bye, Mom," I said, then added "Bye, Kate!"

Kate waved and blew me a kiss. I pretended to catch it and smacked my cheek with it. My heart swelled at the sight of Kate's big smile, then froze when I saw Carleigh standing near the entrance, laughing at me.

My face grew hot. Why couldn't she ever see me doing anything cool? I turned away from her in time to see Alexa step out of her mom's car. She glanced at me and I wiggled my fingers in a wave.

"Alexa!" Carleigh called.

Alexa glanced at me, then at Carleigh. I willed her to pick me, but she turned toward Carleigh and, with an apologetic glance at me, walked over to greet her. *Damage control, right?*

The bell rang, sounding as hollow as I felt.

I hurried to my locker and tried to open it. I still didn't have the hang of it. Twist to the right a few times to clear it or was it to the left? Stop at nine. Spin past the twenty-seven once and stop on it the second time. Then straight to the eleven. I jammed my fingers into the handle and pushed up but nothing happened.

"Do you want help?" Michael asked.

"I think it's jammed, but I don't know. I can never remember how to do it." I handed him the little slip of paper I kept in my backpack with my combo.

Michael got it on the first try. "See you in class." He ran down the hall toward homeroom.

"Thanks," I muttered to him, though he'd already left. I

shoved my backpack and jacket inside and grabbed my English book. The tardy bell rang.

Michael was already sitting at his desk when I plopped into mine a minute after the bell.

"Where's Mr. Black?" I asked him.

He shrugged. "Maybe he's stuck in the bathroom."

I laughed. "When I was a kid, I didn't know teachers even used the bathroom." Why had I said that? I braced myself for him to make fun of me but he didn't.

"I know." He smiled. "I saw Miss Burton at the grocery store one day in second grade. I could hardly believe it. Until that moment, I'd thought teachers lived at the school and never left."

I smiled back. Michael pulled out his English book and started reviewing his homework. I watched him from the corner of my eye. He wasn't popular, by any means. He'd correct the teacher and be right. Most of the other kids didn't like him. Heck, I hadn't liked him when he'd been in my classes in elementary. But maybe he wasn't so bad.

Carleigh and Alexa were deep in conversation at the back of the room. I cursed Sarah for making us late on the first day. Because of her, I'd ended up in the front row of the seating chart.

I pulled out my English book and tried to review my homework. About thirty seconds into it, I stopped. It had been boring the first time. There was no way I could do it again.

The volume of the class rose until even Michael, who could focus through anything, shut his book. Fifteen minutes into class and Mr. Black still hadn't shown up.

"I'm going to go talk to the office," Michael said to me, barely audible over the noise. "Maybe they know where Mr. Black is." He stood up and walked out.

I couldn't believe his bravery.

Another five minutes passed before Michael returned with

Mrs. Lindquist, the receptionist. He hurried to his seat while Mrs. Lindquist called the class to order.

"Pull out your books and read to yourself, please."

"We're working on grammar right now," a boy from the back of the room called.

"No," a girl called, "Mr. Black always lets us sit and talk."

Most of the class agreed, but Mrs. Lindquist shook her head. "Mr. Black isn't here today. I'll be sitting with you until we can find a substitute."

A few kids hissed "Yes!" in excitement.

Michael pulled out a thick book and plopped it on his desk.

"What are you reading?" I asked.

"It's an awesome epic fantasy. This is book seven of fourteen. Each one is about a thousand pages." He smiled. His teeth were white and straight. "What about you?"

I pulled out *Harry Potter*. "I love these. My mom started reading them to me in second grade." Crap. Why had I said that? Would he make fun of me?

"Mine, too. I love those books." His brown eyes sparkled.

"Please read to yourself," Mrs. Lindquist called from Mr. Black's desk.

Michael flashed me one last smile then flipped to the middle of his book and started reading. I couldn't believe how easy he was to talk to. Even when I said or did something awkward, he never made fun of me or laughed at me.

I opened my book and stared at the page. The girl next to me slid a note onto my desk. I looked around. Anna and Carleigh stifled their laughter. My cheeks burned as I looked at the drawing. A girl with holes in her jeans and big lips and a boy with tight, curly, black hair—holding hands—hearts all around them. *Jessa + Michael* was written in bubble letters underneath.

Did I have big lips? Mom called them full and beautiful. But I'd never compared them to anyone else's.

I wadded the drawing up into a ball and tucked my lips into my mouth. The girls snickered quietly behind me. When I glanced back at them, Carleigh puckered her lips.

I put my book on my lap and my head on my desk and pretended to read for the rest of the period.

I TOOK my time putting my books in my locker after fourth period and was one of the last kids in the lunch line. By the time I arrived at the lunchroom, the majority of kids were already sitting down and eating.

"Jessa, want to sit by us?"

I turned around. Michael stood behind me. I hadn't noticed him.

He gestured to a table of rowdy kids. "They're really nice."

"Um," I stalled while I looked for Alexa. She and Carleigh sat next to each other, laughing and eating. Great.

Just then Anna caught my eye. She nudged Carleigh and pointed at me. They both puckered their lips.

Michael tapped my shoulder. "The line moved."

My cheeks burned as I bridged the gap between me and the person in front of me. I grabbed my tray and punched in my lunch number. The line split into two. Michael moved into the other line so he stood across from me at the salad bar.

"So, do you want to sit by us?" He dished lettuce onto his plate.

"Not today," I said, with a glance back at Carleigh.

His smile dropped a little. "Oh. Okay. If you ever change your mind, our table is always open." His line moved and he followed.

"Thanks," I said. My line moved in a different direction. I

stared at the unappetizing food until a girl behind me told me to move.

I finished getting my lunch and found a spot by myself at a near-empty table. The food smelled gross. Michael took his seat with his friends a few tables down, facing me. Farther down the cafeteria Alexa, Carleigh, and Anna sat together. I kept my eyes down, forcing myself to focus on my food. I didn't want to see Alexa laughing at Anna's joke or Michael's broad grin.

"Jessa Newberry, please come to the office. Jessa Newberry."

My name echoed over the intercom. I didn't know why they wanted me, but I had never been more grateful for it. I dropped off my tray and walked out of the lunchroom. I tried hard to not look at Michael as I passed. He and a bunch of other kids played a fantasy card game while they ate. I felt like the whole lunchroom stared at me as I made my way to the doors. I tried to walk slow and measured as I passed Alexa, Carleigh, and Anna, but as soon as Carleigh spotted me, my walk turned into a trot. I could hear laughter behind me but I didn't look back.

Mom stood, one arm leaning on the counter, chatting with the secretaries. As soon as she saw me, she finished her conversations and pulled me into a hug.

I felt a weight off my shoulders as soon as we walked out of the school. "What's up, Mom?"

"I made you a doctor's appointment for the popping in your collarbone. Dr. Lyman is going on vacation tomorrow so they squeezed us in today." Mom opened the passenger door for me.

"I can sit up front?" I crossed my fingers behind my back. I almost never got to sit up front.

Mom winked at me. "S*í, mijta.* It'll be our little secret."

"*Gracias.*" I climbed into the front seat and rolled down the window as soon as Mom started up the car.

The front seat was great. I adjusted my seat a few times.

"How was your day?" Mom asked.

Carleigh and Anna laughing, the drawing, Michael's expression when I'd turned him down, all flashed through my mind. "Okay," I lied.

Mom cocked her eyebrow. She always knew when I lied.

"Mr. Black never showed up this morning," I said to fill the silence. "But the office didn't know. We didn't have a teacher for the first half of first period."

"I hope he's okay." Mom didn't talk for the rest of the drive.

The clinic smelled like antiseptic. We sat in the waiting room for an hour. I wished I had my book. I hadn't collected any of my things before I'd gone to the office. I should have grabbed my backpack at least. Instead I leafed through the children's magazine.

"Someone did all the puzzles?" Mom asked.

At the mention of puzzles, I shut the magazine. "This is for little kids like Kate," I said, and put it away. "I don't like puzzles anyway."

Mom furrowed her brow and opened her mouth to speak as the door opened and the assistant stepped out.

"Jessa?" she called. We followed her back to a room where she took my height and weight while she listened to mom explain why we were there.

Another thirty minutes had passed when Dr. Lyman opened the door. She listened as Mom repeated everything, she'd told the assistant. Dr. Lyman asked me to demonstrate.

I stood up and rolled my shoulders.

Pop. Pop.

"Do it again." This time Dr. Lyman looked at the other collarbone. She touched the hollow under the right side and touched the funny bump under the left side. Her fingers ran up my neck and traced my jaw line. "Hmm... Okay, you can sit back down."

The paper crinkled as I sat on the bed. Dr. Lyman turned to my mom. "There's a few things this could be: a benign bone growth; she could just be sick and have a swollen lymph node. It could also be something more serious. Let's finish up here and we can run a few tests."

Mom furrowed her brow as she looked at me. Was Mom worried about me?

"Should we be worried?" Mom, like a mind reader, voiced my question for me.

"Most likely she's been sick; something her immune system has been fighting without her realizing. We'll do blood work and an X-ray and talk after the results. I'll send you home with an antibiotic to cover all our bases."

Dr. Lyman handed Mom a paper with the orders and a prescription and pulled out a gown for me to put on. "You can keep your pants on under the gown."

"Oh, good. I don't want my butt hanging out when I walk down the hall," I said in relief.

Mom and Dr. Lyman laughed. They both stepped out for me to change, then I joined Mom in the hall. We walked together to the lab.

The lab tech drew my blood without any problems and we went on our way to get the X-ray. I'd had an X-ray of my hand last year after I'd landed awkwardly into a pit of foam at the trampoline park. It hadn't been broken, and they let me keep an electronic copy of the X-ray. I loved to load it up on the computer and look at my bones.

After the X-ray I changed while Mom talked to Dr. Lyman in her office.

"The lump is probably nothing to worry about, but I'll call for sure," Dr. Lyman said to Mom as I emerged from changing.

"Thanks," Mom replied to Dr. Lyman. She turned toward me and smiled. "Let's go."

"Do I have to go back to school?" There were still three hours left. My chest tightened.

"Let's get ice cream and take the day off."

I sighed and climbed back into the front seat.

⁂

SIDNEY SAT, reading her book, when I arrived in Dreamland that night. "I can't wait to beat you in Mario Kart," she said as soon as she saw me.

"Sounds good. I'm ready to have a good dream." I needed to get away from reality. I couldn't think of Alexa or Michael or Carleigh.

Sidney ran to the doorway and leaped out into the open air. I followed, jumping out of the doorway a few seconds behind her. My stomach shot up into my throat as I fell. Sidney made it look easy. I thought of something happy—Michael being nice to me, ice cream and pedicures, playing with Kate. Gravity released me. I shot up next to Sidney and together we flew toward the waterfall. Flying together was easier than doing it alone.

We landed with ease inside the cave, dripping with water and grinning at each other. I led the way through the cave into the room with the fire pit. A ring of boys surrounded it and Sidney waved to them. One of the boys sitting on a log had a shimmery golden glow surrounding him. He looked familiar, but I couldn't place him.

Sidney tugged on my shirt as we walked into the library. I turned around. My clothes still dripped but hers were dry. "Can you dry me too?" I asked. "How do you do it?"

"Just imagine dry clothes and it happens."

I pictured dry clothes and hair but nothing happened.

"Did you see that boy by the fire with the glow around him?" she asked. The smile fell from her face.

"Yeah," I said. "He looks familiar. I think I've seen him before." I closed my eyes and focused hard on dry clothes. The water dripping off my shorts mocked me with each drop.

"He was on the news last night. He drowned." Sidney looked sad.

My eyes flew open. "I don't understand. If he's dead, why is he here?"

Her voice wavered as she spoke. "Sometimes people linger after they die. We all try to be extra nice to anyone with a golden shimmer around them because"—Sidney shifted her weight—"well, nobody knows what comes after Dreamland. We want to make sure they have a good time."

"Oh." My heart felt heavy.

"I'm going to see if he wants to play with us. Is that okay?"

I thought of Dad, always wanting to help the little guy. "Yeah, good idea."

While I waited in the library, I practiced thinking of my clothes as being warm and fresh out of the dryer but nothing happened. Sidney returned with the young boy.

"I'm Danny," he said. His big grin reminded me of Kate.

"I'm Jessa," I said. "Want to play a video game with us?"

"Yeah!" Danny ran down the hall ahead of us.

Sidney took in my still dripping wet clothes and took pity on me. She touched my shoulder and my clothes grew warm and dry.

The Rec Room was half-empty. Danny found an open console and picked out a game. Sidney and I clambered over to the bean bags and started playing.

"Ooh!" We all groaned when Sidney's car spun out and smashed into a wall. Danny easily beat Sidney and me. After we lost to him a few times, another girl asked to race him. She looked about his age. Sidney and I handed over our controllers and moved away from the consoles to a comfortable couch.

I couldn't stop looking at Danny. "We might be the last people to ever see him."

Sidney nodded and...flickered.

"What's happening?" I asked. "You disappeared for a second."

"I'm waking up," Sidney said. "I'll be back, but if I don't see you, do you want to come over to my house tomorrow?"

"Yeah, I'll come right after school," I said.

"See you then." She flickered again then disappeared.

I spent the rest of the night watching Danny beat anyone who played him. Though he'd beaten me and Sidney, I had a feeling the older kids he won against would've creamed him on a normal night. Tonight, though, everyone around him wanted to make sure he went out on a win.

Chapter 7

The next morning a stout, round woman holding a Diet Coke stood at the front of class when we walked in. Mrs. Lee explained she would be the substitute until Mr. Black could return.

Michael asked her where Mr. Black was, but she ignored him and taught the lesson. The rest of the class tried to take advantage by telling Mrs. Lee all sorts of lies like Mr. Black never made the class read and always let us out of class five minutes early. Mrs. Lee didn't listen to any of it. I liked her, but only a handful of the class shared this opinion. Before long most of the class had been given detention.

At the end of the day, Alexa caught up with me at my locker after the bell to go home.

"What's up with you and Michael?" she asked.

"What are you talking about?" I put my Spanish book in my bag and dug around for my Math book.

"Carleigh said he's your boyfriend. Why didn't you tell me you liked him?" she asked in a wounded voice.

"I don't like Michael!" I exclaimed. "We're not even friends." I needed to squash this rumor before it gained more force. "And you haven't been around for me to talk to, anyway."

Alexa blushed. "I'm still working on Carleigh," she said in a small voice.

I looked up just as Michael walked past. My stomach

dropped. Had he heard me? He hurried past us, eyes focused on the ground.

"Great," I muttered under my breath. I slammed my locker and started walking toward the door leaving Alexa by my locker.

"Jessa, wait up." Alexa jogged up to me and, without breaking stride, looped her arm through mine and started walking with me. "I'm sorry it's been so long since we talked. I've missed you. Mom wants me to invite you over more. I don't think she's a fan of Carleigh or Anna. Last time they were over..." Alexa launched into a story about what Carleigh had said to Alexa's mom.

I stopped listening. My anger deflated into hurt. She'd had Carleigh and Anna over but not me. And her *mom* wanted me over? I tried to slow down, but Alexa didn't notice. She kept her arm looped through mine and marched me out the doors.

"Anyway, I've missed hanging out with you. I keep trying to convince Carleigh that you're cool and fun to hang out with. If I can get her, then Anna will follow; she does everything Carleigh does." Alexa said all this without stopping for a breath. She inhaled and continued. "Do you want to come to the mall after school? Carleigh and Anna will be there when they get out of detention. It'll be good for your image if you can be friends with the three of us." Alexa stopped and turned toward me. "What do you say?"

"I'll need to ask my mom." A thought tugged at the back of my mind. Did I already have plans this afternoon?

"Not a problem. Here." She handed me her phone. I punched Mom's number into the text app. Mom knew my schedule. She'd tell me if I had a prior commitment.

This is Jessa. Can I hang out with Alexa after school today?

We waited. The bubble with three dots appeared—she was texting me back.

Sure. Be home by dinner.

Thanks.

Alexa smiled and snatched her phone back. "It'll be fun. Let's hang out here until they get out of detention then my mom will pick us up." She looped her arm back through mine and we walked over to a tree by the front of the school. She slipped her arm out of mine and we both sat down in the shade.

Had Alexa or Mrs. Johnston invited me? The thought made my heart sink. Why did everything have to change?

I felt even worse a moment later when Michael walked past. He didn't look at me, but I had the feeling he'd seen me.

Fifteen minutes later, Mrs. Johnston pulled up in her white SUV and rolled down her window. "Jessa, honey, it's good to see you," she called when we approached.

"Mom," Alexa moaned. "Don't be embarrassing."

"Sorry, sweetie."

Alexa rolled her eyes.

"Good to see you too, Mrs. Johnston." I smiled but I didn't really feel it.

Alexa's phone buzzed and she looked down at it and held her index finger up. "Hang on, Mom." She read the text. "Carleigh is coming right now."

I climbed in the middle row of the SUV and waited. Alexa stood with the door open, watching the front doors of the building.

Finally, Carleigh and Anna came out. My insides squirmed. Maybe this would be okay. Maybe we *could* all be friends like Alexa thought.

When they got to the SUV the two of them and Alexa squished into the back row leaving me to sit alone.

Maybe not.

Mrs. Johnston dropped us off at the mall and told Alexa to call or text if we needed anything.

"Let's go check out the shoes," Carleigh said after we walked in.

"Yeah, I love shoes," Anna said.

"Okay, but I want to look at dresses too," Alexa chimed in.

I didn't say anything. This was way beyond me. My experience was strictly with thrift and discount stores. We shopped in the clearance rack during the off season so we could afford the clothes.

The three girls forged ahead as I trailed along behind catching snippets of their conversations.

When we stopped at the shoe store, they went straight to the women's section and each grabbed a pair of strappy high heels.

"I can't believe Drew wants to be your boyfriend," Alexa exclaimed as she pulled on the little panty-hose socks the store provided. "He's *so* cute!"

Carleigh slipped on her black heels and walked down the shoe aisle. She spun in a circle at the end and didn't even wobble. "I told him I'd have to think about it."

"What? But you totally like him," Anna said as she struggled to untangle the straps to the heels she'd picked out.

Carleigh walked back down the aisle as though she were walking down a runway. The heels made a perfect *click clack* with each step. She stopped in front of me and looked me up and down. "Try these, Jessa." She took the shoes off and handed them to me then turned to Anna. "I do like him. But I don't want him to *know* I like him."

I took the shoes and dug out a pair of the nylon socks from a box on the wall.

"That doesn't make any sense," Anna said. "Don't you want him to be your boyfriend?"

The nylons somehow barely covered my feet yet bunched around my toes.

"Of course she does," Alexa piped in. "But you don't *tell*

them. They have to work for it, right?" She looked up at Carleigh for verification.

Carleigh nodded. "Plus, I think Jaden likes me, too. I'm not sure who I like more."

I slipped on the heels. *I'm going to make a fool of myself.* But I stood up anyway.

Alexa sighed. "Jaden is pretty cute." She turned toward me. "Those are adorable, Jessa! Take a turn." She held her hand out indicating I should walk down the aisle.

I took a breath and a step. My feet slid in the shoe until my toes mashed together at the point. I couldn't make the heels *click clack* the way Carleigh did. Mine dragged with each step. When it came time to spin around, I didn't dare. Instead I turned around and shuffled my way back to them. At least I hadn't fallen.

I looked up at Carleigh's wide eyes. Her hand covered her mouth, trying to hold in her laughter. Anna snickered.

Alexa frowned at Anna. "Maybe those are a little big for you, Jess," she said, and the kindness in her voice helped me relax a little.

"It's like you're a little kid playing dress-up." Carleigh let out her laugh, and Anna joined her.

Alexa grabbed a smaller size and walked them over to me. "Try these."

I slipped the smaller pair on and took another walk down the aisle. I managed to not wobble too much, though my heels still didn't clack the way that Carleigh's did. I sat back down as Anna took her turn.

"Who do you like, Jessa?" Carleigh asked.

I shrugged, slipping my shoes back on. "Nobody, really."

Anna spun like a ballerina and walked back to us. "Is it Michael?" she asked.

"No," I said with an edge to my voice. "I don't like anyone."

"Riiight." Carleigh dragged out the word and her tone suggested she didn't believe me.

"Let's go look at the dresses," Alexa said, putting her shoes back in the box. She checked her phone. "My mom will be here in forty-five minutes."

We walked to a dress shop and Carleigh grabbed a cute dress with a high waist and soft flower print. "Jessa, this is perfect for you. You *have* to try it on." She shoved it into my arms and the other girls agreed.

When I stepped out of the dressing room Anna came up to me first. "You look stunning in that dress! You should totally buy it."

Carleigh came over. "Wow, I *love* it! How much is it?"

I glanced at the price tag long enough to know I'd never be able to afford it.

"Try this one on next." Anna put another dress in my hands.

I spent the rest of the time letting the other girls choose my outfits for me. All the clothes they picked for me in my size were much looser than usual. They told me over and over how cute each outfit looked on me. It made me feel good, but I didn't understand why they were mean one second and nice the next.

When Alexa's mom picked us up Anna sat up in the middle row with me. Maybe I was making progress. I probably *had* looked like a toddler playing dress-up in the heels Carleigh had handed me. Was this how middle school girls interacted with each other? Maybe the hot and cold was normal.

DINNER WAS ALMOST ready when I came home. Kate set the table while Sarah helped Mom in the kitchen. Dad sat in the living room surrounded by ropes, carabiners, and harnesses, sorting and organizing our climbing gear like he did every autumn.

"Dinner's ready," Mom called to Dad.

I helped Sarah bring dinner to the table. We sat down and started eating. While Sarah and Dad conversed about Sarah's upcoming driver's license test, Mom looked over at me. "Sidney called today. She seemed disappointed when I told her you weren't home."

The food lost its flavor in my mouth. I'd accidently blown off Sidney to hang out with Alexa. Would Sidney understand?

I set my fork down, and I must have looked upset because Mom said, "Are you okay?" and put her hand on my shoulder.

"Can I go see Sidney after dinner?"

Mom gave me a scrutinizing look. "You just spent all day with your friends. Don't you have homework?"

"Please, *mamá*? It's the weekend. And I spent the day with Alexa, not Sidney." I paused, wondering how I could change her mind. "Sidney is alone and sick. I promised her I'd stop by tonight." Mom's face softened. I pushed a little more. "Please? I don't have any homework. Pretty please?"

"I think it's a great idea," Dad chimed in. "Sidney's dad told me how lonely she is. She could use good company...goompany?"

"No," we told him in unison.

Dad made a face. "I think it'd be good for both of them."

If Dad was convinced, I'd won. He'd talk Mom into it.

"Well..." Mom hedged, "Okay. Let me ask Sidney's mom if it's a good time for a visit."

"Maybe we can make her family a treat!" Kate squealed.

Dad cleared his dish. "Great idea."

"No-bake cookies!" Kate cleared her dish too and started digging through the recipe box. She couldn't read most of the recipes to find the right one, but the No-Bake cookie recipe was so faded and dirty from use, it was easily recognizable.

"You're joking," Sarah said, still sitting at the table. "Why does Jessa get to ditch her chores all day and hang out with friends?"

"This isn't a social call. You're welcome to go and visit any of your sick friends." Dad's tone was mild but challenging. "If Jessa made a promise to see Sidney, she needs to honor it."

"I made a promise to go to Vienna's today and help her dye her hair," Sarah whined. "Mom made me break it by keeping me home to do chores and homework."

"That's not the same," Dad said. "Sidney is seriously sick."

Sarah gave me a scathing look before stomping upstairs. "This is so unfair."

I sighed and Dad gave me a half smile and said. "Sarah will get over it."

Mom got off the phone. "We can head over around seven. They're eating right now."

"Jessa, I can't read this," Kate said, holding up the faded recipe. I leaned down and helped her sound out the words.

How would it be to see Sidney in real life? My stomach fluttered. What should I say to her? Would it be as easy to talk to her in real life as it was in Dreamland? I hoped she'd forgive me for not going over right after school.

Kate and I scooped out the cookies onto a waxed cookie sheet and put it in the fridge. At 6:45 we put a plate together and all piled in the car—except Sarah, who was still pouting in her room.

Mrs. Thatcher answered the door. "Thanks for coming," she greeted.

"Hannah, how are you?" Mom hugged Mrs. Thatcher.

"We're getting along." She spoke into Mom's hair. They

pulled apart. "What's this?" she asked, bending down to Kate's level.

"We made them for Sidney!" Kate exclaimed happily.

"She'll love them." Mrs. Thatcher opened the door and we followed her inside.

The Thatchers' house was clean but cluttered. Mom, Dad, and Kate stayed in the front room while Mrs. Thatcher showed me to Sidney's room. A large butterfly sticker still covered her door.

I felt like I'd been thrown back in time when we walked into Sidney's room. Sidney had always loved butterflies and her room had been covered with them since kindergarten. Her room looked almost the same now as it had then. The biggest difference were beads strung across her walls like tinsel and the box of medical supplies next to her bed.

Sidney lay in her bed, eyes closed. My insides twisted. She looked so different from how she looked in Dreamland. Here she was pale and bald. A tube led from a tank next to her bed, wrapped around both of her ears, and rested near her nose. Her eyes looked sunken in and so did her cheeks. Her thin, frail arms were wrapped around a stuffed elephant.

"Sidney? You have company," Mrs. Thatcher said.

Sidney opened her eyes.

"Hi," I said, feeling awkward. I didn't know how to start this conversation.

"I'll leave you girls alone," Mrs. Thatcher said, and stepped out of the room.

"I didn't think you'd come." Sidney raised her hairless eyebrows but smiled. "Can you sanitize your hands, please?"

"Sure." I squirted the sanitizer on my hands. The smell of rubbing alcohol assaulted my nose. I wasn't sure what to say. Why was it easier to talk to her in Dreamland? I took a couple steps into the room and sat down on a chair. We sat in silence for a few minutes. I looked at the ceiling. Dusty paper butterflies hung on beaded strings from the ceiling.

"Those are cute," I said, pointing at the butterflies.

"Do you recognize them?" She asked.

I looked closer. "No way. Are those the same butterflies we made to decorate your room in Kindergarten?" I laughed.

"The very same." Sidney's eyes twinkled.

The rhythmic whoosh of the oxygen tank filled the silence.

"I went back there today," Sidney said after a few moments.

"You can go during the day?"

Her eyes shone bright. "Any time you fall asleep."

"Huh. I can only go sometimes, not even every night."

"It takes practice. I've been going there for a long time." Sidney fiddled with a beaded bracelet on her wrist.

She seemed shy in real life. The Sidney from Dreamland was spunky, adventurous, and outgoing. "Did you see Rafa and Lauren?" I asked.

"Only Rafa. It seemed emptier than usual."

"That happens sometimes, right?" I asked.

Sidney shrugged. "I don't know. This feels different, but I don't know why."

"Let's check it out tonight," I said.

Sidney nodded, but still seemed uneasy.

I looked at the nearest string of beads next to me. They were all different shapes and sizes. "I like your beads."

"Thanks. I get them from the hospital. Each bead represents a treatment or procedure I've had done." She indicated the bracelet she always wore. "These are my favorite."

"That's a lot of beads." I looked around at all the beads with a new found respect.

Sidney smiled weakly. "Well, when you have cancer three times in six years..." She shrugged.

We settled back into silence. I couldn't believe all of the

procedures she'd had. I leaned closer to one strand and saw a faint glow coming off of a few of them. "Are these glow-in-the-dark?" I asked.

She didn't answer. I turned toward her. Her eyes were closed and her head was back on her pillow. I took a step back. I didn't want to wake her if she'd fallen asleep.

Mrs. Thatcher popped her head in the door. When she saw Sidney resting, she motioned me out of the room. I stood and walked to the door.

"Thanks for coming," Sidney half moaned, half whispered from across the room.

When I looked back over, she appeared to already be asleep.

"Is she going to be okay?" I asked Mrs. Thatcher when she'd closed Sidney's door.

"The treatments are hard on her, but her last scans looked good, so we're hopeful."

I crossed my fingers and held them up. Mrs. Thatcher smiled and copied the gesture.

Mom and Kate waited for me by the front door while Dad stood in the kitchen still talking to Mr. Thatcher.

"Thank you all for coming." Mrs. Thatcher looked down at Kate. "And thank you for the cookies. Those are Sid's favorite. She'll be happy to have them when she wakes up."

"We'll try to come by again soon," Mom said as she ushered us out of the house.

Chapter
8

My eyes had hardly closed when they opened in Dreamland. Sidney lounged in her usual hammock in the tree house reading a book. Her tanned skin and her short, spiky hair gave a sharp contrast to the Sidney I'd seen in real life. I hadn't realized just how sick she was. How did she change her appearance?

She looked up at me and put her finger in the book to hold her place. "Thanks for coming over. Sorry I fell asleep at the end."

"No problem," I said.

Sidney stood, folded the corner of the page, and dropped the book into the hammock. She walked over to the massive trunk. "Check this out." She pointed to a long, black gash cutting across the trunk.

I stepped closer to examine it. The gash was as long as my arm and half as deep. A sickly-sweet smell of peppermint lingered in the air around it. The edges looked crispy and burnt. But inside the gash looked wet, slimy, and rotten.

Sidney's eyebrows furrowed. "I've never seen anything like this before. It's kind of freaking me out," she admitted, looking at the floor.

I didn't know much about this place, but I could tell when someone was scared. Sidney had enough happening in real life; she didn't need to be scared here too. I took her hand. "I'm sorry you're scared."

She smiled but not her usual huge, contagious grin. I smiled as big as I could and crossed my eyes. We both laughed.

"Let's go play," Sidney said.

We flew down to the hideout. Sidney was right, there were fewer kids here. Had something happened to them?

We found Rafa lounging on a recliner in the Rec Room, one leg flung over an armrest, the other resting on the floor. He wasn't playing a game or watching the others play. He just stared up toward the dark cave roof.

Sidney gave me a worried look. "Hang on, okay?" She touched him lightly on the shoulder. "Rafa?"

He started and looked around. "Huh? Oh, hey, Sid." He turned his gaze toward me. "Hi...Jess, was it?"

"Jessa."

He didn't seem to hear me. Sidney grabbed an ottoman and pulled it up beside the lounger. "What's wrong?" She touched his arm. I squished onto the ottoman beside her.

"I haven't seen Lauren in a few days." He sat up and clasped his hands together. One of his knees started bouncing up and down.

Sidney squeezed his arm. "That's normal. Sometimes I don't see people for weeks."

Rafa nodded, eyes downcast. "Yeah, but she's usually here every night. I'm just...worried, I guess. What if something happened to her in real life?"

"Maybe she's getting better?" I chanced.

"Maybe." Rafa nodded but didn't look convinced.

Sidney turned toward me, her brows furrowed, for a moment. Then her eyes widened and she smiled. "C'mon, I've got the perfect thing." She jumped up and pulled on Rafa's arm a little.

Rafa looked up at her but didn't move. "What?" His tone was pensive.

"Let's go fly in the clouds." Her smile widened.

"Yeah," Rafa said, finally smiling.

"What's in the clouds?" I asked, my insides twinging with excitement and the prospect of an adventure.

"You haven't been there yet?" Rafa asked.

I shook my head.

Rafa's jaw dropped and he turned toward Sidney. "We *have* to show her."

"Show me what? What's in the clouds?" I asked.

Sidney laughed. "You'll see."

"The clouds were my gift." Rafa said as we walked to the door.

"You mean, what Dreamland made for you?" I asked.

"Yeah," Rafa answered.

"What'd it give you, Sidney?" I asked.

Rafa slowed and turned toward her. "Yeah, what *did* it give you? I don't think I know."

Sidney shrugged. "Don't worry about it right now. I'll show you guys later."

"How did you know it was yours?" I asked.

"You can't miss it," Rafa said. "I felt something pulling me toward the clouds. Almost like the clouds themselves were calling me. I followed the tug. When I got up near the clouds, the air around me was cold but as I moved closer, I felt warm all over, like I had stepped into a warm shower. I just *knew* it was mine."

We started walking toward the library. "What about you, Sidney?"

She shrugged. "Pretty much the same. I saw something glowing off in the distance, so I flew there. When I landed, I had the same warmth shoot through me. I think it's that way for most kids here."

"Did you find your gift, yet?" Rafa asked.

I shook my head.

"I saw a new bridge by the little river in the forest. Maybe that's yours." Rafa said.

"And the zipline is new," Sidney added.

"I think I'm here as a fluke. I mean, I'm not sick or anything," I said feeling a little guilty I could access Dreamland while still healthy.

Rafa smiled. "I hope you're right, but sick or not, you've been here enough times that Dreamland would have made something for you." He lowered his voice to a theatrical, sinister tone as though he was telling stories around a campfire. "Legend says if you don't find your gift, you could accidentally make your own thing. But it's a dark and twisted version that hurts other kids. You know the cave in the cliffs, way on the north side of the island? It used to be the home of a dragon some kid created. He thought it would be cool, but then the dragon terrorized the island until one day it straight up ate this girl's unicorn and choked on the horn."

"That's enough ghost stories for now, Rafa," Sidney laughed. "Glad to see you're feeling better already. Let's go." We'd made it to the exit. She and Rafa flew out first. The waterfall pushed me down as I followed and I came out the other side dripping but dried off after a few minutes of flying. The warm rays of the sun shone down through the clear blue sky. Big white puffy clouds sat high in the sky. The cool air rushed past us as we flew.

Thick, dark clouds loomed on the horizon in the distance. I blinked and shook my head. One of the clouds looked almost like a pirate ship.

Rafa flew ahead putting on bursts of speed one moment then flying in lazy loops the next. Sidney hovered and waved for me to catch up. I flew past her and she laughed. We raced toward Rafa, who disappeared into one of the biggest clouds.

Sidney pushed ahead of me and disappeared soon after.

The cloud looked wispy but strangely solid. I flew to the place where Sidney and Rafa disappeared. I stopped in confusion. A path had opened up in the clouds. I looked around for signs of Sidney and Rafa but didn't see them. They must have gone in. I let myself glide inside. The breeze stopped and the temperature dropped a little. As I flew farther down the path, the entrance behind me closed.

The walls looked like fog. Maybe I could fly through them. I reached out to see if they were solid or not. My hand disappeared in the mist past my wrist before I hit something solid but soft and spongy. My hand was damp when I brought it out of the cloud.

The mist swirled around me as I flew down the path, making it hard to see anything. The path came to a T. Was this a maze? I looked up and could see the sky above me but there was no other way to orient myself.

"Sidney? Rafa?" I called.

"Over here!" Sidney called.

I turned toward her voice...off to the left? I followed the passage turning corners until I ran into a dead end. "Sidney?"

"Jessa, up here," Sidney said.

I looked up. She floated high above me.

I flew straight up until we floated next to each other, above the clouds. Below sprawled an enormous maze made of clouds. The paths shifted as we watched, opening and closing in different places as the wind blew.

Rafa flew toward a big circle in the middle of the maze.

"A cloud maze?" I asked Sidney.

"Yeah! It's pretty fun. You can work your way through or fly above it." Sidney started flying toward Rafa. "C'mon, you'll love this," she called over her shoulder.

I followed them. The enormous area looked about the size of a couple of football fields.

White, puffy benches lined the circular area. Hundreds of topiaries made from clouds decorated the space. Flying above I spotted a horse, a spider, and a tree.

"C'mere Jess!" Sidney called. She and Rafa waited for me near one of the benches next to a topiary shaped like a bear.

When I landed, my feet sank into the mist up to my ankles before they settled on the soft and springy ground. I felt like an astronaut walking on the moon. With each step the ground pushed me higher and farther than normal.

"This is wonderful!" I said when I made it to them.

Rafa smiled. "The perfect distraction." He reached over to the bear, tore a chunk out of it, and popped it in his mouth.

Sidney did the same.

I reached into the mist and tore a chunk of the springy material away. It came off easily. I took a bite. The piece of cloud melted into sugary sweetness when it touched my tongue. "Cotton candy!" I exclaimed. "It's berry flavored."

Sid ripped a piece from a cat topiary next to her and took another bite. "Isn't it great? They're all different flavors, too."

I tore off a piece from a dragon topiary and popped it in my mouth.

"Ew!" I spit it back out. "Hot sauce."

"Try this one," Sidney said. She stood by what looked like a giant bee.

I took a small piece and tried it. "Honey, yum." I pulled off a bigger piece and ate it.

The three of us moved around trying different flavors until we'd tried them all.

We sat on one of the benches looking at all the shapes all around us. Rafa pointed to one of the topiaries. "I think that's a dog."

"No way," Sidney said. "Look at the schnoz on it. It's clearly an anteater."

"Jessa?" Rafa asked. "Which do you think it is?"

"Sorry," I said to Sidney, "it looks like a dog to me too. I mean, look how long the legs are, and the way it's standing..."

"Oh, come on," Sidney laughed. "You're both blind. It's an anteater."

We debated several different shapes until Rafa sighed. "Thanks for suggesting this, Sid. It's exactly what I needed."

Sidney smiled. "Give it time. Lauren will be back soon."

"I'm going to go check again." He stood up from the bench, flew into the air, and waved to both of us as he left.

"Isn't this great?" Sidney stood and twirled around, dancing to her own music.

Something had been bothering me, though. "Shouldn't the sun be setting soon?" I asked.

Sid twirled a few more times than stopped. She put her hand on the side of a large pirate ship for balance.

"Sunsets are rare, but they stick around longer than real sunsets. I don't think nighttime ever truly comes. I've seen twilight several times. It'll linger for a few hours before the sun rises again." She walked over next to me and grabbed a piece of the truck topiary I stood next to.

I took a piece of the truck, popped it into my mouth, and enjoyed the chocolate flavor.

"What happens to the clouds up here when it rains?"

"The rain falls below the clouds, so the cotton candy is safe. Rain doesn't happen often and when it does, it's a light rain and brings triple rainbows." She walked to a bench nearby and sat down. "The weather is almost perfect; the sunsets linger for hours...it's paradise."

"What an incredible place." I said, sitting down next to her.

She leaned up against me and put her head on my shoulder. "Yeah. I never want to leave."

THE WEEKEND FLEW BY, and by Monday morning, I woke up feeling like nothing could bring me down. The weekend had been the break I'd needed from school. I barely noticed Anna and Carleigh in the corner laughing and glancing in my direction and I didn't care when I sat alone at lunch again. I couldn't stop thinking about Sidney and Dreamland.

When we got home from school, I helped Kate make a piece of toast. Mom walked in from the car, her eyes empty and watery. She dropped onto a bar stool next to Kate, not even bothering to shut the door to the garage.

"Are you okay?" I asked.

Mom shook her head like she was trying to get the thoughts out of it. "Yeah. Dr. Lyman just called from her vacation."

My stomach clenched. Was something wrong with me? "And?" I asked, trying to keep my voice steady.

"They want to take the lump out."

I didn't see why this was so bad. "Okay..."

"They wanted to remove it as soon as possible." Her eyes were still unfocused.

"Do you think it's bad?" I tried to keep the worry out of my voice.

Mom blinked and looked down at Kate who had finished her toast, her face and fingers now sticky with jam. "Go wash up, sweetie," she said to Kate.

Kate huffed and stomped off. She'd probably try to lick all the jam off rather than washing it.

"Mom? Is it bad?" I sat down in the chair next to her.

Though I couldn't feel the lump, I imagined it pulsing inside me.

"I don't know, *mijita*." Mom finally focused on me and shook her head. Her voice turned harder and more business-like. "Dr. Lyman said she doesn't feel comfortable doing the surgery, so we will be heading up to Children's."

"What?" I asked. "Why?" Was this more serious than Mom was letting on?

"She said you'll be in better hands with a pediatric surgeon. I called Children's and they were able to squeeze you in tomorrow." She stroked my hair and pulled me in and kissed me on the forehead. "It's probably nothing."

But what if it's something?

Chapter 9

As I lay in bed, I couldn't stop thinking there might be something wrong with me. Mom was worried. After tossing and turning for hours, I finally drifted off.

I found Sidney in the library, reading on a bean bag. A few other kids milled about. Sidney put her book away. "Hey, Jessa. I assumed you weren't coming tonight. What took so long?"

"I couldn't fall asleep."

"Are you okay?"

I looked around. I didn't want to talk to her about it in front of the other kids. "Can we go somewhere?"

Sidney smiled. "I have the perfect place." She grabbed my hand and led me out of the hideout. We flew through the waterfall and high up into the sky. I could see the island spread out below. The sun reflected off the bright blue water.

We flew over the forest toward the mountain. The air chilled my face as the sun warmed my back. The trees looked as small as pencils and the island itself looked no bigger than my table at home. The dark clouds in the distance spun and shifted from one shape to another. Was that a pirate ship again? It looked almost the same as the one I'd seen on the way to the cloud maze.

"Do you see that?" I pointed to the clouds. But Sidney started into a spiral dive. She spun like a cork screw for several seconds before looping back around to fly next to me. I smiled but I didn't feel it in my heart.

When we approached the mountain, Sidney dove and I followed. The trees on the mountain came closer and closer until the ground came close enough, I could have reached out and touched it. We weaved through the trees, following a small stream until the ground leveled out.

Sidney stopped abruptly at the tree line. I flew past her straight into the middle of a wildflower-covered meadow. The colors were so vibrant they didn't look real. When I landed, the flowers rose up around me as hundreds of butterflies flew into the sky.

As I turned back around, Sidney made her way toward me through the meadow. The butterflies she disturbed fluttered around her, then landed back on the grass.

"Wow." I took in the sweeping view of the ocean. "I thought all those butterflies were flowers." I turned to Sidney, expecting to see her big smile, but she wore a frown instead. "What's wrong?"

She swept her hand out in front of her indicating the grassy meadow. "The flowers are gone."

"What?"

"Every time I've been here before, it's covered in wildflowers. The smell is amazing. I used to come and lie in the sun, surrounded by flowers, and watch the butterflies flutter around me." She sat down in the dry grass, looking shaken.

"Is this what Dreamland gave you?" I sat down next to her.

She nodded. "I haven't shown it to anyone in all my time here. It felt too personal."

My heart swelled. I couldn't believe she had shared this with me.

We both looked around. The grass was green—but not as green as I'd first thought. Big patches of brown were more prevalent after the butterflies had taken off.

"What's happening to this place?" she asked.

I couldn't answer.

I woke the next morning to Dad gently shaking me.

"Jessa, c'mon. It's time to get up."

"What time is it?" I grumbled.

"It's 4:30. We have to get going if we're going to make it up to Children's in time." Dad stroked my hair. "We're all ready to go. You don't need to even get dressed. Mom's packed an outfit if you want to change later."

I stretched. "What about breakfast?" I asked.

"Remember, you can't eat or drink anything until after surgery. We talked about that last night," Dad reminded me.

"Oh, yeah," I sighed.

Dad scrunched his nose. "You can brush your teeth though."

"Daaad." I tried to infuse it with as much morning breath as possible.

He laughed and pulled me into a quick hug. His suit coat scratched my face. "Why are you all dressed up to go to the hospital?" I asked.

Dad sighed. "I'm sorry, bug. I'm heading on a trip today, remember? I'll be out of the country for a couple of weeks. I can come to the hospital with you, but I have to leave after they take you back to surgery."

This wasn't new. Dad had been traveling internationally for as long as I could remember. But he'd always managed to make it to all the big events. "You won't be there when I wake up?" A pit formed in my stomach.

"I'll make it up to you," he promised.

"How?" I challenged. I put a smile on my face to let him know it was okay, even though my stomach felt like I'd swallowed a rock.

"How about a Daddy-Daughter date when I get back?"

"A Dadterate?" I tried.

"I don't think that works." Dad laughed.

"What will we do on our date?" I asked.

"I could take you climbing," Dad offered.

"And dinner?" I countered.

"How about climbing with ice cream after?" Dad asked.

"Sounds greaaat." I breathed more morning breath on him.

Dad made a face and flopped over on my bed as though dead. When I poked his side, he caught me in his arms and tickled me. I laughed and squirmed away.

"Be down to the car in twenty." He gave me a wink and walked out my door.

After a quick shower and teeth brushing, we pulled out of the driveway. I had the middle row of the van all to myself.

I pushed my pillow up against the window. The drive was about an hour and a half. I wanted to go back to sleep, but my mind buzzed with questions and worries. I had never had surgery before. What if I didn't wake up? What if something happened during the surgery? And the most daunting question —the one I wouldn't let myself examine—was this lump the reason I could go to Dreamland? Would I still be able to go to Dreamland after the surgeons removed it?

I woke up when we pulled off the freeway and stopped at a traffic light. The sky was lighter and the clock read 6:32. I'd managed to sleep the whole way.

"Good morning, Jessa." Mom smiled back at me. "How are you doing?"

I could see the anxiety behind her smile and I felt the same way. I shrugged, trying not to let my nervousness seep through.

My stomach growled audibly.

"Hungry?" Dad asked.

I nodded.

"Sorry. You'll be able to eat after the surgery." The car pulled forward and Mom turned her attention back to navigating.

We passed through the city. I couldn't help watching the people around us. What were they worried about today? Was this an ordinary day for them? Just heading to work and school?

Time slipped past, and before I was ready, we'd arrived at the hospital and the assistant was leading me back to a room.

Two nurses came into the room both dressed in green scrubs with surgical hats on. One stepped forward; his hand extended. "I'm Eric," he said, shaking hands with Dad. He was a head shorter than Dad which put him eyelevel with Mom. He had a neatly trimmed beard. "We're about ready to go. Dr. Shubert is finishing up his last surgery, so we need to prep Jessa, and we'll head back in about ten."

"I have a question," Mom said to Eric.

I didn't hear the rest because the other nurse came over to me. "I'm Becky and I'm going to get an IV started, okay?" Her soft and gentle voice helped calm me a little. She was young but I could see silver strands of hair poking out from her surgical hat.

"Okay," I said, my insides in knots.

Becky squatted down beside my bed. "I'm going to find a vein first."

I nodded, too nervous to speak.

Her cold hands made me shiver.

"Sorry, the O.R. is cold, so whenever I come out my hands are cold too." Becky smiled. "That's what we call the operating room for short," she added. With a soft touch, she pushed on my right arm a few times, looking for a vein. "Are you doing okay today?"

I shrugged. My dry mouth felt glued shut and I could feel tears trying to form behind my eyes.

"It's okay to be nervous. I'm pretty good at IV's. Have you had one before?"

"No," I said, and my voice cracked.

Becky tied the tourniquet tight around my arm above my elbow. "We slide a tiny tube into your vein. It helps us put medicine into your body while you're asleep."

I nodded again. My throat felt tight. I wanted to fly away from all of this. So many thoughts were flooding my mind. *What if they find out there's something wrong with me? What if the scar is huge and never goes away? What if I never wake up? What if I can't get to Dreamland after this?* Again, I could almost feel the lump inside my body, pulsing.

Becky lined up her supplies. "Are you ready?"

Mom came over and sat on my bed, holding me in a hug. Tears slipped from my eyes and ran down my face.

"Here's a pinch," Becky said.

Pain shot up my arm and I cried out. Mom held me steady.

"Don't move, Jessa, or she'll have to do it again," Mom whispered.

My arm burned in the crook of my elbow where she worked.

Dad grabbed my other hand and squeezed it. "You're doing great, kiddo. She's almost done."

I could feel Becky doing something to my arm. Was that tape?

"This will be cold," Becky said.

A cold sensation shot up my arm.

"Okay, all done."

Mom released me and moved to her chair.

"How does it feel?" Becky asked. "I put a little cover on it so you don't have to see it. It shouldn't hurt anymore now that the needle is gone."

A little brown sleeve covered the IV site. She was right, it didn't hurt anymore. In fact, the more I thought about it, it hadn't been that bad. It scared me more than it actually hurt. "It feels okay. Really cold, though," I said.

Becky smiled at me as she hung up the IV bag at my bedside. "That's the fluid we're giving you. It'll be okay. I'll be in the O.R. with you. Dr. Shubert is the best."

"Thank you," Mom said as Becky exited the room.

Mom handed me her phone. "Why don't you play a game while we wait?" I pushed the button to check the time. At seven-thirty I'd normally be eating breakfast and getting ready for school.

School. Alexa. I hadn't told her I'd be gone today.

"Mom, can I text Alexa?"

Mom and Dad were talking to yet another person in scrubs —a grizzly bear of an old man.

Mom waved and nodded but didn't look over.

Have fun at school today.

I waited. Would she answer me or was she busy?

Three dots appeared inside a text bubble. She was responding. **Are you not coming? Where will you be?**

I thought for a minute. Should I tell her everything? Or just about the surgery? **Eating ice cream and pudding.**

The dots appeared again. **Jealous! Does your mom know?**

I laughed. **Lol. Having surgery today. I'm up at Children's. Be home tonight.** I waited for her response but nothing came. **Come visit tomorrow?**

Mom came over and took the phone from me. "They're ready for you." She kissed my forehead.

I wished I could take the phone to distract me. Panic rose up inside of me.

The big man who'd been talking to Mom and Dad came over to me. He stood a head taller than my dad and was two times as large. His fuzzy beard covered his face, merging seamlessly with his chest hair.

"I'm Dr. Draper. I'll be your anesthesiologist. Let's get this cap on your head." He pulled out a blue, almost see-through hat and put it on me. "I'm going to be here with you the whole time. I'll make sure you're safe, okay?"

"Okay." I wanted to jump off the bed and run out of the hospital.

Someone released the brake on my bed and they rolled me forward. My stomach felt like I'd swallowed a dozen trampoline artists and they were putting on their best show.

Mom grabbed my hand and Dad touched my head.

"I'll see you in a little bit, Jessita." Mom squeezed my hand so tight I was glad she'd grabbed my non-IV hand.

Dad leaned down and kissed my forehead. "I'm leaving in a few minutes for the airport. I love you."

The trampoline artists each did several triple flips.

"Love you too, Dad."

"Come on. Time to go," Dr. Draper said. He pushed my bed out of the room and down the hall.

The ceiling tiles flashed past over my head. The IV made my whole right arm feel like I'd packed it in ice. I shivered.

"Are you cold?" Dr. Draper asked.

"I'm not used to wearing just a gown," I tried to joke.

Dr. Draper smiled and slowed the bed down. "Hang on." He left me for a minute and came back with two warm blankets.

I sighed as the warmth spread through my body. "This is my favorite part so far."

Dr. Draper winked down at me. "It's my favorite part, too." He tapped his badge against a square on the wall and a set of double doors opened. He turned a few more corners, leaving me completely disoriented. He stopped the bed and pushed a button to open another door.

"Here we are," he said.

The air got even colder in the operating room, but the blankets kept me warm. The stark room felt empty but had a lot of equipment in it. Several people bustled around the room preparing things. Everyone wore surgical hats and masks.

My stomach tightened. The trampoline artists jumped higher and harder.

Dr. Draper put a blood pressure cuff on my arm and another monitor on my finger. The machine behind me started beeping.

Becky came in and smiled at me. At least I think she smiled —I couldn't tell through her mask. She laid another warm blanket on me.

"I'm going to put this mask on your face to help you get all the oxygen you need, okay?" Dr. Draper put a soft rubber mask over my mouth and nose.

I could feel the air hissing in through the mask. The monitor beeping sped up.

"I want you to count backward from ten." Dr. Draper said.

"Ten..."

Cold shot up my arm from the IV.

"Nine..."

Instruments clanged on the other side of the room.

"Eight..."

My head felt lighter. Everything felt funny. I started laughing uncontrollably.

"Seven..."

VOICES. Laughter. Beeping.

Something squeezed my arm, hard.

I cried.

The laughter stopped.

"Jessa?"

Mom? Her voice sounded miles away.

"Jessa, are you awake?"

I tried to respond in words, but only groans came out.

The thing squeezed my arm again. I didn't like it.

More beeping.

The skin near my collar bone burned.

I started crying.

"It's the medicine. It's hard to wake up sometimes," a female voice said.

"Is she okay?" Mom asked.

"Give her time," the female voice said.

I tried to open my eyes, but my eyelids felt heavy.

"Okay," Mom said.

I felt her hand on my arm and relaxed back into sleep.

I HEARD THE BEEPING FIRST. The steady rhythm made me think of a metronome. Beep. Beep. Beep. Beep.

A whirring noise started, and something squeezed my arm, tight. I tried to roll over to my right side, but pain shot up from my chest. I moaned.

"Jessa?" Mom asked, touching my right arm.

My eyes fluttered open. Where was I?

"You're awake." Mom kissed my forehead. "How do you feel, *nena*?"

I was in a hospital... Why was I here? My brain struggled to come up with the answer.

"Mom?" I groaned. My throat was on fire.

"I'm here." Mom stroked my hair.

I looked around as best as I could, trying to clear the mud from my mind. The room looked different from before; instead of walls, a curtain formed a room around my bed.

A nurse pulled it back and entered. "It took a little while to wake you up. How are you feeling, Jessa?" She didn't wait for an answer. "Can you try to eat a spoonfull of ice?"

I groaned. My eyelids felt like weights were attached to them. I wanted to go back to sleep.

Mom took the cup and scooped up a bit of the crushed ice onto it. "Open up, Jessita." She moved the ice-covered spoon toward my mouth.

I obliged. The ice soothed my throat and also helped clear up some of the muddiness in my mind.

"I'll be back in a few. Would you like pudding or cookies? We have crackers, too," the nurse said as she pushed a button on the blood pressure machine. That's what squeezed my arm.

"Yes, please," I croaked. Talking hurt.

Mom spooned more ice into my mouth.

"Your throat might hurt a little. They put a tube down it to help you breathe, which is normal," the nurse said. "I'll be back in a minute with pudding and Jell-O. Sound good?"

I nodded, and she pulled the curtain back and left the room.

Mom set the cup down and held my hand. "You did great. The doctor said they got the whole thing out. It'll take about a week for the biopsy to come back, but for now, it's over. We don't have to worry about it, okay?"

"Biopsy?" I asked.

"They look at the lump and tell us if it's cancer or not," Mom said. "If it's malignant, that means it's cancer. If it's benign, that means it's not."

I nodded.

The next few hours seemed like a blur. I ate Jell-O and pudding and cookies. I drank a cup of water. When I got up to pee, I wobbled so much Mom helped me walk to the bathroom and sit on the toilet. I felt embarrassed, trying to pee with her there but she turned her back and gave me privacy. When I was ready to go, dressed and discharged, they wheeled me to the car and helped me climb inside.

Chapter
10

Falling asleep was easy. I felt loopy and sleepy from the pain medicine Mom gave me. My head barely hit the pillow before I opened my eyes in Dreamland. Sidney waited for me in her usual hammock.

"Hey, Jessa!" She cocked her eyebrow and asked, "What's that on your chest?"

I looked down. A big bulky bandage covered my collarbone. "Oh... I had to get...something removed today." I couldn't say the word *lump*. I tried to adjust my shirt to cover the bandage. "I just got home from Children's tonight."

"You were at Children's?" Sidney remarked. "I wish I would have known. Maybe I could have visited you."

I dropped down on the hammock next to her. "I was pretty out of it." All the stress of the surgery hit me and I needed to talk to someone about it. I knew Sidney would understand, but I couldn't get the words out.

"You can make it go away, if you want."

"Huh?" I asked. How could I make a sickness go away? "I don't even know if anything is wrong with me yet."

Sidney's eyes widened. "I was talking about the bandage." She pointed at the bulky dressing. "You can change things about yourself by thinking them away, remember? Like drying your clothes." She screwed up her face in concentration. Her tanned skin paled, her hair receded, and soon she looked like the sickly, bald Sidney I visited a few days ago.

"Wow," I said.

"Just imagine what you want to look like. It takes practice and concentration."

I closed my eyes and imagined what I'd look like without the dressing. I opened them and looked down. Just my night shirt and no bulky bandage. "Can I look like whatever I want?"

"The more you change, the harder it is to hold on to your true image. I've been coming here for so long, it's almost harder for me to project the true image of myself." Sidney closed her eyes and she changed back into the Dreamland Sidney I'd become accustomed to.

"Can you change into anyone?" The possibilities excited me.

Sidney's eyes lit up. "I've never tried." She closed her eyes. Her hair grew longer and changed in color to match mine. Her eyes grew a bit bigger and moved a little closer together. Freckles sprouted across her nose, exactly like mine. Her clothes changed and before I knew it, I was looking at myself.

She hopped up and walked to the end of the tree house. A mirror now hung on the previously empty wall. Had she created it?

We stood side by side staring at the mirror; she was an exact replica of me. "Whoa," we said in unison. After a second, her facade faded and she turned back into herself.

"That was hard to hold on to," Sidney said.

I concentrated on changing my dark hair to blonde. Nothing happened. I closed my eyes and thought harder. When I opened my eyes, my hair was still the same color. "How'd you do it? I can't even change my hair color."

Sidney shrugged. "Maybe it's easier to turn yourself into someone you know rather than change something about yourself." She plopped into a hammock. "Like, it can be hard to picture yourself with different features but it's easy to know what someone else looks like."

"You don't look like yourself in real life," I said. The instant it came out of my mouth, I wanted to take it back. "I'm sorry—that's not what I meant," I stammered.

Sidney looked away but didn't respond. My apology hung in the air for a moment before turning into uncomfortable silence.

I closed my eyes and sighed. I felt like such a jerk. I sat down in the hammock next to her. "Sidney," I reached out and touched her arm, "That came out all wrong. I'm sorry. I'm just —" I didn't want to say it, but it spilled out of my mouth in a rush. "The doctor removed a lump and my mom's worried, especially because they wanted me to get surgery as soon as possible. We only found out last night that they wanted to remove it." I shifted in the hammock. The hammock's seam underneath my legs dug into my skin. "I'm just freaked out. But I shouldn't have said that," I finished.

"It's okay." Sidney's voice sounded small. "I know I look different here. But I look how I feel inside. I don't feel like I should be a pale, bald girl who can hardly sit up. I don't have to think about the mouth sores and bed sores and fevers here." She sounded exhausted. She stood up and raised her hands as if displaying the world around her. "Here, I'm *not* sick. Here the way I feel about myself is reflected in my appearance. Here I feel safe, I have fun, I can just *be* without having to worry about being sick and treatments and everything." She dropped her hands. "I'm not sick here. I'm just me."

I stood up and hugged her. "I'm really sorry."

"It's okay." She pulled away from me after a moment. "Are you okay? That sounds scary."

I couldn't put into words the anxiety I felt about all of this. My eyes started to burn and a lump rose in my throat. I couldn't trust myself to speak so I shrugged.

"I know what you mean," she said. And I knew she did.

She hugged me again. When we pulled apart, our eyes brimmed with tears. Sidney wiped hers with the back of her hand. "Enough of this nonsense. Let's go flying."

I nodded and ran to the doorway. "First one there gets to choose the game!" I jumped out of the doorway, letting myself plummet for a few seconds before flying up above the trees. Sidney was right behind me, laughing.

MOM KEPT me home from school for the rest of the week after surgery. I didn't have any more Dreamland dreams, despite how much I tried. After three days of TV and a weekend of slow recovery, I was ready to go back to school Monday. Alexa texted me a few times telling me she couldn't come over—she'd been grounded.

Mom came into my room at bedtime Sunday night and sat down on my bed. Her eyes were narrowed with concern. I could tell we were about to have a serious talk. Had she heard from the doctor? I braced myself for the worst.

"Jessa," she touched my arm the way she always did when she tried to sooth me. "I don't think you should go back to school tomorrow."

I let out a breath I hadn't meant to hold. Before I could speak, she rushed on.

"The doctor said you need to rest and—"

"Mom!" I whined. "I've been resting for five full days now. I can't take another day sitting here watching TV. I can't get behind in school." And I needed to see my friends.

"You only missed three days of school, and Sarah brought you the work you've missed. You should be okay."

"Pleeeeease," I begged. I felt trapped and antsy.

Mom sighed and bit her lip—sure signs she was changing her mind.

"How about if I go a half day? I'll call you if I don't feel well and you can come and get me." I wrapped my arm around her and put my head on her shoulder. "Pretty please?"

She looked down at me and smiled. "You know, your dad wants you to stay home."

"Wait, I can go?" I asked.

"Yes. Take the kids' phone with you."

"Thank you!" Relief washed over me. I gave her a one-armed squeeze and a peck on the cheek.

"I expect you to send me text updates."

"Of course. Thank you, thank you, thank you!"

Mom kissed the top of my head and stood. "Listen to your body and take care of yourself."

"Yes, ma'am." I lay back on my bed, smiling as Mom walked out of the room.

IN THE MORNING I awoke to a door slamming downstairs. My bed was soaked with sweat again. I had tossed and turned all night long, trying desperately to get into Dreamland. I missed Sidney.

After a quick shower I came downstairs, looking for Mom and Kate and Sarah but nobody was home. The clock read 8:10. Mom was probably taking Sarah and Kate to school. I sighed in frustration. *She'd said I could go.*

My stomach felt like a giant knot. I hurried and dressed, then made a piece of toast even though nothing sounded appetizing.

Mom walked in the door and put her keys and purse on a set of hooks. "You're up." She smiled.

"Why didn't you wake me?" My annoyance came through in my tone.

"You needed all the rest you could get. We can head to school whenever you're ready."

"I'm ready right now." I glanced at the clock; 8:30. I'd have to walk in with the whole class watching. My stomach twisted harder. I suddenly didn't want to go.

"All right." Mom gave me a half smile. "You're a strong girl, *mijita*."

I half shrugged—it still hurt to move my shoulder very much.

After too much fussing and Mom asking me three different times if I'd taken my morning pain medicine, we finally made it to the school. My resolve waned. Maybe one more day at home wouldn't be bad.

Mrs. Lee sat in the back of the class with a giant Diet Coke in her hand. The only noise came from the scratching of pencil on paper. A few kids looked up long enough to stare at me as I walked to Mrs. Lee and handed her a tardy slip.

"You'll need to get your class journal out. I want you to write a paragraph about what you did this weekend."

I nodded then took my seat.

Michael touched his foot to the leg of my chair to get my attention. I turned toward him.

"Where have you been?" he mouthed.

Mrs. Lee cleared her throat.

"Later," I mouthed back.

He nodded.

When English finally ended, Michael walked out to our lockers with me.

"Where have you been?" he asked.

"Sick," I half-lied. I didn't want anyone to know I'd had

surgery, though I wasn't sure why. "Any news about Mr. Black?" I asked.

"Not officially." Michael shook his head.

"Wait, do you know where he is? Even my mom doesn't know, and she subs Spanish for the school all the time." We stopped by my locker. I twisted the lock and tried to pop it open but it was even harder with my sore shoulder.

He shut his locker and waited, watching me struggle for a minute before—

"Here." He nudged me aside after I'd done the combo. Pushing his math book into my arm, he banged on the corner of my locker again and then popped it open.

"Thanks," I said, keeping my eyes on my locker. For some reason, my heart had sped up and I felt more awkward than usual.

Michael hadn't noticed and continued talking. "My cousin Rafael has been in a coma for years. He's in a hospital with a long-term care facility. On his same floor is an inpatient mental hospital. We visited him this last weekend, and I saw Mrs. Vanderbilt in the hall—"

"The principal?" I interrupted.

"Yeah. She and Mrs. Chi were talking about Mr. Black and how he's had a mental breakdown. He was so sad about Mrs. Black; he's stopped functioning and now lives at the hospital until he gets better." Michael started twisting his lock.

"Wow." How would it feel to be so sad that you stopped functioning? I put my English book into my locker and grabbed a note from Mom for gym class and my copy of *Harry Potter*. "I hope he gets better soon. Can he get better?"

Michael shut our lockers and we both started walking toward the gym. "Yeah. My mom said he'll have to go to therapy and they'll give him medicine and stuff."

"Wait, did you say Mr. Black is in a mental hospital?"

Carleigh stood next to us. She'd come out of nowhere. "So, he's like, crazy?" She had a smile on her face like this was the funniest thing she'd heard all day.

"He's not crazy, he's just very sad," Michael said.

"Did they put him in a straitjacket?" She laughed, but Michael and I didn't.

"It's not funny," I said.

"It's not his fault his brain chemistry is off," Michael said. "Mental illness is the same as any other illness. If you had an infection, you'd go to the doctor and get antibiotics. It's the same idea."

"Whatever." Carleigh rolled her eyes. She turned down a different hallway.

"She's such a jerk," Michael said. "Why do you want to be friends with her?" he asked. We both started down a set of stairs.

"I don't know. She's Alexa's friend, and Alexa and I are best friends. She's not that bad of a person." But I heard the lie as it came out of my mouth.

"She's a bully. She and Anna and all their little friends. You deserve better friends." He slowed down as we approached the gym doors. "Want to eat lunch with me?" The question came out in a rush and his voice jumped an octave on the last word. He cleared his throat and kept his eyes on the ground.

I stopped and turned toward him. "I—" I started. My cheeks burned.

"Jessa!" Alexa ran over and pulled me into a hug that squished my incision site.

I pushed her off. "Ouch."

"Oh my gosh, I'm sorry! Is that where you had surgery?" She grabbed my hand and swung it back and forth. "Doesn't matter. I just talked to Carleigh. You're in to sit with us at lunch!" Alexa's smile stretched across her face. "Isn't that great?"

I forced a smile back but glanced at Michael. He hadn't moved, but he wasn't looking at his feet anymore. His eyes locked with mine. I couldn't read the expression on his face. Disappointment? Hurt?

"That sounds good," I said, breaking Michael's gaze.

Alexa laughed. "Great, I'll save you a spot. I gotta go now or I'll be late for class. See you at lunch." She turned and walked down the hall.

The bell rang. I turned toward the gym door in time to see it swing shut. I couldn't stop picturing the look on Michael's face. I'd been wanting to be friends with Carleigh since before school started. So why did I feel so awful?

Chapter
11

At lunch I couldn't stop glancing at Michael. He sat with his usual table of friends, but his head was down and he wasn't talking to anyone. Alexa and Carleigh invited me to hang out with them after school, but I turned them down. My incision ached—the medicine hadn't helped. I was tired. When Mom texted to check in with me, I told her I was ready to go home. She came right away and even carried my bag to the car.

When we got home, I went straight to my room and crashed. I fell asleep the moment my head hit the pillow.

I woke up in Dreamland.

The pain from my incision disappeared, and I felt well rested. Having the contrast of feeling awful in the real world and feeling great here was eye opening. No wonder Sidney loved it here. She was so sick in real life.

I jumped from the tree house and flew through the cool air toward the hideout. Sidney would probably be in the Rec Room. As I flew over the waterfall, I stopped and hovered. Sidney sat alone on the rocks where the mermaids usually sunned themselves.

"Hey." I landed next to her. "What are you doing out here?"

"Bad day." Sidney didn't look up.

The cool mist around us made me shiver. "Want to talk about it?"

Sidney stood and scooped up a handful of pebbles which

she started tossing into the water one by one. Her hair stuck to her head, and her clothes were damp and wrinkled.

"I had a scan last week, and things don't look good. The tumors aren't going down like they should."

I scooped up my own pebbles, stood next to her, and started tossing them into the water.

"What does that mean?" I wanted to hold my breath.

"The chemo they're using isn't working, so they need to change my treatment plan. I might have to spend more time at the hospital." Sidney tossed the last pebble from her hand and dusted her hands off on her shorts.

I threw all of mine into the water. The pebbles made tiny splashes. I shivered. A light rain started falling, chilling me even more. "I'm sorry." I wiped my hands clean and pulled her into a hug.

When we broke apart, she sniffed. "It gets to me sometimes. It's just a lot, you know?"

I nodded. Goosebumps rose on my arms and I rubbed them to try and warm up.

"You're freezing. This weather is crazy." Sidney shivered then smiled at me. "Let's get hot chocolate and warm up."

I followed her through the waterfall and into the hideout. I concentrated on dry clothes and was surprised when it worked.

Sidney led me off the main room and into a little passage I hadn't seen before. After a short walk, warm air welcomed us into a cozy room no bigger than a trampoline. A table with cups and mugs sat on one side of a small bubbling brown pool. Steam rose from it in waves. Another table with marshmallows, spices, and liquid flavorings sat on the other side of the room.

"It's a lava hot chocolate spring," Sidney explained with a smile.

We dipped and filled our mugs with warm cocoa, then

moved to the toppings table. I gave mine a shot of vanilla syrup and sprinkled cinnamon on top.

Sidney put a shot of hazelnut in hers, then grabbed a handful of marshmallows to top it off. She walked to the doorway and sat down on a puffy chair. A table with card games sat between the two chairs. I sat next to her and we wrapped ourselves up in blankets, sipping our cocoa.

"Why didn't I know about this?" I asked, taking another sip. "I love hot chocolate."

"The weather is usually perfect. I don't know how many stormy days I've ever seen here. Most people don't want hot chocolate on a warm day."

"This is the best hot chocolate I've ever had." I finished my mug and set it on the counter. "Do we wash it?" I asked, unsure what to do with my dirty mug.

"It's already clean," Sidney said.

I looked back in the mug. All evidence of hot chocolate was gone. "No dishes," I said, putting the cup back on the table. "I love this place!"

Sidney still looked troubled as she sipped her drink.

"Are you okay?" I asked, looking through the card games on the table.

She shrugged. "Scans aside, I'm still worried about Dreamland. Especially with the weather being weird." Sidney set her mug down.

"Is there anything we can do about it?" I asked. "You'd know better than anyone."

"I don't know," Sidney said.

"We'll figure it out," I said, picking up one of the games. "Do you want to play a game?"

Sidney smiled. "Okay."

THE NEXT DAY, school dragged on. My incision ached all day, but I wanted to stick it out. Alexa invited me to sit with them at lunch for the rest of the week, and Carleigh and Anna didn't seem to mind. I tried to smile at Michael during science, but he never looked my way. Was he mad at me?

An announcement from the office interrupted our test. "Please send Jessa Newberry to the office. She will be leaving for the rest of the day."

"Okay," Miss Harper, my science teacher, replied. "Grab your things. You can finish the test on Monday."

A couple of the kids in the back of the class groaned with jealousy. Michael finally looked over at me. I smiled at him. His tentative smile made me feel a little lighter as I walked to the office.

Mom stood waiting for me. Her eyes were red and she sniffed a few times before grabbing a tissue off the office desk.

My gut twisted. "Is everything okay? Did someone die?" I blurted out.

Mom shook her head and pulled me into a long, careful hug. "We need to go to see Dr. Lyman."

My stomach sank. "Is it bad?"

Mom grabbed my hand and pulled me along. "I don't know, *chiquita*. I'm worried."

The drive to Dr. Lyman's office seemed to take longer than usual. Neither of us spoke. I rolled down my window to relieve the oppressive silence inside the car. The cool September air flooded in, and I let it blow over me.

Mom parked and we went into the office together. I sat on a floral chair next to Mom in the waiting room. She gave my knee a squeeze. The assistant finally called my name. She didn't take my weight or even take us to a room; she took us straight to Dr. Lyman's office.

Dr. Lyman came in a few minutes later. "Thanks for

coming." She sat down at her desk. "I got your biopsy results back from the pathologist."

I shifted in my seat. This didn't bode well. My chest felt tight and empty.

"And?" Mom asked. She sat on her chair as still as a statue.

I held my breath and wiped my sweaty palms on my jeans, willing Dr. Lyman to say everything was normal. But deep down, I knew.

"It's Hodgkin lymphoma, which is very treatable." Dr. Lyman's gaze was sympathetic as she waited for my response.

"What does that mean?" Mom asked.

I wasn't sure I understood, so I didn't respond.

Dr. Lyman leaned forward. "It's cancer of the lymph nodes."

"Oh," was all I could say.

A buzzing filled my ears.

Mom put her arm around my shoulders and pulled me closer to her. Dr. Lyman still spoke but I only heard the buzzing.

How could this be happening to me?

I wished Dad were here.

Cancer.

I thought of Sidney and how awful she'd felt in real life. Would I have to go through chemo too? Would I lose my hair? Why me?

Cancer.

Would I miss a lot of school? What would everyone at school say?

I needed to talk to Sidney.

Cancer.

Like a bad song, I couldn't get the word out of my head.

Chapter
12

I was in a haze for the rest of the day. Mom spend all day either on the computer researching Hodgkin's disease or on the phone talking to everyone from the insurance company to *abuela*. Dad video called me and apologized over and over for not being there. He assured me he was on his way home tomorrow, which was a whole week early, so he could be there for my scans.

Dr. Lyman had explained that my lymph nodes were supposed to fight infection. She told me about all the scans they'd do to figure out if the cancer had spread and which stage I had. She told Mom to take me back to Children's to see a specialist because they'd know exactly how to treat me. She listed off symptoms that can come with Hodgkin's, and I confirmed a few of them: night sweats and loss of appetite. All because I had...

I couldn't say it anymore. I couldn't think about it anymore. I needed to go to Dreamland. I needed Sidney.

She'd gone through this three times now. What kind of cancer did she have? Something to do with her brain? Or was it bone? I felt like the worst friend.

Alexa and Mrs. Johnston dropped by that evening with a dinner for the family. Mom thanked her and invited them in.

Mom and Mrs. Johnston talked for a half hour before Mrs. Johnston said they needed to leave. Alexa had sat next to me and played on her phone the whole time. I couldn't believe that she wouldn't even look at me. Right before they left, she reached out like she wanted to hug me, but settled for an awkward shoulder squeeze and an "I'm sorry."

"It's fine," I said as they left.

Mom pulled me into another hug after we'd walked them to the door. "It's okay, mamá. I'm okay."

But why did I keep saying that?

I had told everyone over and over that it was okay. That *I* was okay.

But I wasn't.

I PACED THE TREE HOUSE, hoping Sidney would show up soon. But after a few minutes of pacing, I had to get out of there. Feeling reckless, I threw myself out of the door and let myself free fall. I tried to think of something happy but came up blank. I thought of Kate, snuggling against me when she was sad. Or Sidney and I exploring Dreamland together. But neither of those thoughts worked. The ground was coming closer. What always made me happy? What did I want most right now?

I wanted to see the stars. I wanted the feeling that came with looking into space and knowing how big the universe was. The vastness of the universe always made me feel small. And maybe feeling small right now could make this problem feel small.

It worked. I launched myself up above the trees and hovered in the air. Warmth spread from my head to my toes and fingertips. And then I felt a small tug, like someone had placed a string around my heart and, ever so gently, started pulling on it. I was ready for whatever Dreamland had made for me.

Closing my eyes, I let the feeling guide me through the sky. The wind blew past my face, and I opened my eyes to see a flash of light on top the mountain up ahead. Excitement bubbled in my chest as I flew closer and closer to the glowing mountain top.

Would it be something fun and entertaining like Rafa's cloud maze? Or maybe something peaceful and serene like Sidney's meadow?

The grass tickled my legs as I landed. At the highest point in Dreamland, in the middle of a natural clearing, a new, white building sparkled in the sun. I walked toward it, feeling the pull even stronger now. The building was a little smaller than my classroom at school. The domed top looked like it retracted.

A heat flashed through my body that left my arms and legs feeling tingly as I approached the stone steps that led to a wooden door. The building had just one circular room inside. In the middle of the room sat a telescope that rivaled what I'd seen at the planetarium. One long tube of the telescope stretched up toward the ceiling. A few shorter tubes were attached to the side of it. The whole thing was mounted on a platform in the middle of the room. I stepped closer to it and noticed several knobs and switches near the eye piece.

Dreamland had given me an observatory. My heart felt like it was ready to burst.

I looked into the telescope and everything was black. Of course I couldn't see anything. There was probably a cover on it, and the dome wasn't even open. I examined the knobs and switches near the eyepieces and found a switch labeled Dome. I flipped it.

A motor whirred and the dome above me started to open. I looked around, wishing I had a star chart, when I noticed the walls were a painted star chart that I could use to locate the constellations and planets.

Light spilled in from the opening dome, breaking through my excitement and turning it to disappointment.

Dreamland was perpetually in daylight, making my observatory utterly useless.

My heart shattered.

Why would Dreamland give me something I couldn't even use? It had to be a mistake.

I looked through the knobs again, reading the labels carefully until I came to a switch that puzzled me. The top was labeled Day and the bottom Night. The switch pointed up toward the Day section. I flipped it.

A beam of darkness shot out of the telescope. But not darkness, exactly. It was as though the telescope could pierce through the sunlight and show what the world would look like at night. The inside of the observatory dimmed and I felt like I was on my patio looking at the stars.

The walls around me gave off a faint light and, as I stepped closer, I realized the star chart was glowing. Each star and constellation glowed faintly in the dark. I looked into the telescope and focused it by turning the eyepiece.

My heart felt like it stopped. The Milky Way was spread out before my eyes. I had never seen anything so beautiful before. I turned another knob, and the platform that the telescope sat on rotated. I searched the sky, zooming out to find Cassiopeia and Camelopardalis. Once I located them, I zoomed in on Camelopardalis. I could finally see all the stars in the constellation.

What else did I want to see?

The Andromeda Galaxy?

I found Cassiopeia again and followed the bottom of the 'w' down to just before the Pegasus constellation. It took me a minute to switch between the different eyepieces so I could locate it. But when I saw it, my breath caught.

The door opened behind me, casting outside light into the room.

"Jessa?" Sidney asked. "Are you in here?"

I turned around and stepped off the platform. "I'm here." My voice was low and calm.

"What is this place? Is this your gift from Dreamland?" Sidney stepped into the room and shut the door, letting the room shift back to the dim lighting.

"It's my observatory," I said. Seeing Sidney brought back the reality of my diagnosis. Tears pricked behind my eyes. I took a slow, steadying breath.

Sidney walked closer to the telescope. "May I?"

I stepped back. "Go ahead." My voice sounded small.

She leaned up and looked through the eyepiece. "What am I looking at?"

"The Andromeda Galaxy." My mouth felt dry. "It's the closest galaxy to ours.

"Wow," she whispered. After a moment she pulled herself away from the telescope.

I wanted to tell her about my diagnosis, but my mouth wouldn't form the words. Instead I asked, "How did you find me?"

Sidney pointed to the beam of night shooting from the observatory. "It's like a searchlight. Hard to miss."

"Except it's not a light. It would be a search-night," I said with a half-smile.

Sidney laughed. A comfortable silence fell between us as we both stared into the sky. Sidney was the first to break it.

"Your mom called my mom this afternoon." Sidney looked me straight in the eyes and I felt a strength from her I'd never noticed. "I'm so sorry, Jessa."

Words failed me. What was I supposed to say?

I looked away and shrugged. "It's okay," I said automatically.

"No. It's not okay, Jessa. It sucks." She took a step forward and put her hand on my shoulder. "If you don't want to talk about it, we don't have to. But I know what you're going through."

A lump rose in my throat. The world around me started to blur as my eyes filled with tears. "I'm scared," I admitted.

"Me too. Why do you think I'm here all the time? This place has saved me." She smiled. "I'll always be here if you need me."

I sniffed and nodded. "Thanks."

She sighed. "Want to look at the stars with me? You can show me your favorites."

"What have you always wanted to see?" I asked.

"Saturn," Sidney said without hesitation.

Once I found Saturn on the star charts on the walls, I turned the telescope in that direction, locating the planet easily. After zooming in on it, I stepped back and let Sidney have a turn. My chest felt looser after talking to Sidney. Mom was right; everything was easier with a friend.

Chapter 13

The next day, Mom and I drove to the airport to pick up Dad. Dad gave me a big, long hug. When he pulled away, he wiped his eyes. Then he pulled Mom into a tight hug and whispered into her ear. She cried onto his shoulder, getting his suit coat wet. Dad held her head and pulled me into their embrace.

I had a few tests scheduled for that day and the next at Children's so we had brought our overnight bags and planned to stay at my *abuela's* house.

I still didn't know how I felt. Scared? Sad? Angry? Mostly, it didn't feel true. How could *I* have cancer?

I hadn't been allowed to eat so they could do all the tests today. Thankfully I could have lots of water.

In the radiology department, a few kids and their parents sat in the waiting room. The light blue walls were painted to look like water with coral and seaweed painted along the edges. Colorful fish completed the paintings, giving the overall impression of being in an aquarium. Did an aquarium like this exist in Dreamland?

After we signed in, Mom and Dad sat on either side of me on the padded waiting room chairs. A couple of kids were sitting at tables, coloring or playing with toys. Mom put her hand on my knee and squeezed. Dad pulled me into a side hug and kissed my hair.

All their affection irritated me, but I didn't know why. Each stroke of my hair and squeeze of my knee or pat on my back made me angry. I wanted them to stop looking at me and feeling sorry for me. I wanted to be left alone. I wanted to be invisible.

I could feel Mom and Dad looking at each other behind my back and doing their silent communication thing. Mom stroked my hair again.

I stood up in a rush, trying to hold back my frustration, and turned to face them. "I'm going to go color."

Mom's eyes were rimmed with unshed tears but smiled at me and nodded. Dad scooted over to my vacated seat and pulled Mom into him.

Coloring did not sound fun, but I didn't know how else to get away from them while we were all trapped in the aquarium waiting room.

The table was made for toddlers to sit at, so I knelt next to it. A pile of papers sat in the middle. I grabbed the top sheet, which was a picture of a fish and a mermaid, and started coloring. I colored the mermaid with pink streaks in her hair and an aquamarine tail.

We waited for a long time. Once in a while, an assistant opened the door and called out a name. Then a kid and their parents would follow her through the door. Had I seen any of these kids in Dreamland before? How would I know? If they changed their appearance like Sidney, I might never know.

Several more families joined us in the waiting room until all the chairs had filled. I was still coloring at the toddler table, but there weren't any seats next to Mom and Dad anymore. My stomach growled. I took a sip from my water bottle to ease the hunger pangs. I wanted to get this over with so we could go home.

"Jessa?" the woman called. I jumped up, leaving my picture behind, and walked over to her. Mom and Dad followed close behind.

"Follow me."

We walked down a hallway with similar aquarium decor until we arrived at a private room. "Jessa, I want you to change into this gown. Your parents and I will wait outside." She handed me a gown that looked three sizes too big. "When you're done, flip this light switch and we'll come back in."

I nodded, and she shut the door.

The oversized gown was like a tent. I wasn't sure whether to take my underwear off or leave it on. I decided to keep it on. She could always tell me to take it off later.

After I flipped the switch, I climbed up onto the crinkly paper and waited.

The door opened and everyone came in.

"Okay, Jessa." The nurse sat down at the computer and typed in a password. "You're going to have a PET scan. We will have to put in an IV so we can inject radioactive tracers into your body."

"What?" I asked. "I have to have radioactive stuff injected inside me...on purpose? Will they give me a super power?"

The nurse laughed. "No. Don't worry, your body removes them naturally. Make sure you drink plenty of water to help flush them out," the nurse said with a smile. "The PET scan will help us see where the cancer is inside your body. Did you have food today?"

I shook my head.

"Do you have any questions?" She gave me a warm smile.

I shook my head again. "No."

"Great." She stood and walked over to me. A small metal table, with various medical supplies on it, sat next to my bed. She started opening the little packages and putting everything together.

I gave Mom a worried look, and she pulled out her phone

and handed it to me. I pulled up my favorite game and tried to ignore the rest of the world.

The IV pinched and burned, but she got it on the first try. The medicine gave me a weird taste in my mouth.

"We have to wait for ninety minutes for the radioactive tracers to get into place. Then we'll be back to take Jessa to the scan."

My stomach growled again. The nurse left. Mom pulled up a movie on her phone. I tried to watch and forget about what was happening, but I couldn't get the thought out of my head about having something radioactive running through my veins. I'd had X-rays before, but something felt different about having a radioactive liquid inside me.

After a little while, Dad sat down next to me. "I stayed in this hospital for a few weeks when I was young."

I paused the movie. "What happened?"

"When I was about nine, I caught a bad virus. Grandma took me to the hospital. I was in the ICU for a week, and then I spent another week recovering."

"What was it like?" I asked. I'd never heard this story before.

"I don't remember a lot." Dad's eyes seemed a little more distant and he gave a chuckle. "I think I played a lot of Space Invaders." He shook his head. "Anyway, what I'm trying to say is, I know it's scary, but you'll get better. Okay?"

"Thanks, Dad." I pushed play on the movie and continued watching.

The movie was almost over by the time the nurse came back in. She took me into another room where I had to lie still on a hard, slim table.

Once I was in place, the table slid into a huge machine shaped like a donut. The machine spun around my body, quickly at first, but then it slowed down. The radiologist played music to distract me, but it didn't help. I could move some of the time but other times I had to hold completely still. As soon as the radiologist would tell me to hold still, I'd get a deep itch and not be able to scratch it.

After a long thirty minutes, the scan was over. They kept me on the table for a little while longer while they made sure the tests had worked and they wouldn't have to redo them.

While we waited, a nurse brought out a clear plastic container. Inside were beads—like Sidney's beads in her room.

"Have you heard of the bead program?" the nurse asked. She held the container out for me to look through.

"Yeah, my friend has some. Don't I get one every time I have to do something like this?" Each section held a different color of bead. They all had a washed out look, but as she tilted the container, the beads in the shadow glowed. "Are they glow in the dark?"

"Yes. Is this your first bead?"

I nodded. Did I want pink or purple? I dug through the container and found a glittery white that reminded me of a star in the night's sky.

"Hang on." She handed me the container and stepped out of the room. She returned with another plastic organizer full of beads. "Let's get you all set up."

The new container held alphabet beads. The nurse helped me pick my name out of the letters, then together we made the starting of a bracelet.

I slipped it on my wrist. "It's a little bit pathetic," I said, holding it up for the nurse to see.

"These beads represent the first steps to remission." The nurse looked me in the eyes. "With each bead, you'll be one step closer to being cancer-free."

"The beginning of the end?" I asked.

"Only if it's the end of cancer." She winked at me.

ABUELA GAVE me cookies and hugs and Grandpa made dinner and played cards with me. Mom let me text Alexa, but she never responded. Maybe she was grounded from her phone or maybe she was too busy with Carleigh and Anna.

As I lay in bed trying to sleep, Grandpa and Mom walked past my room. I feigned sleep—I didn't want to talk to anyone. They stopped at my door.

"When does she start treatment?" Grandpa asked.

"We hope next week, but maybe in two weeks," Mom said.

"How is she doing with all of it?"

"She's kept to herself. I think it helps that she has a friend who is also going through cancer." Mom sighed. "The doctor said it takes two to four weeks of chemo for her hair to start falling out." Her voice broke on the last word. "I don't know what to do. I looked into wigs, but they're so expensive." She took a slow breath in and exhaled. "Little girls shouldn't be bald."

Bald. The word hung in the air like the note after a gong. It chilled me to my bones.

I cracked my eyes open. Mom had one arm wrapped around herself and the other covering her mouth. Grandpa reached over and pulled her into a hug.

Mom turned into his shoulder and started crying in earnest. They shut my door, leaving me alone in the dark. I closed my eyes and tried to sleep but I couldn't get the image of Mom crying out of my mind.

When sleep came, Sidney was waiting for me in the tree house. She didn't say anything, but she pulled me into a quick side hug. "You okay?"

"Yeah. I have my CT scan tomorrow. We're at *abuela's* right now," I said.

"Do you want to talk about it or anything?" Sidney asked. Her concern felt genuine and comforting.

"I want to have some fun." I didn't wait for her answer. I grabbed her wrist and pulled her to the edge and jumped off, still holding her hand. We flew together, and it was as if I left all my problems in the tree house. Even though she couldn't do anything to fix the problem, Sidney's understanding always helped me feel better.

The dark sky made it hard to see, and the wind blew us off course more than once. The rain had us soaking even before we flew through the waterfall.

My damp shorts stuck to my legs as we walked into the hideout. The floor sloped up and I was looking down when I ran right into Sidney.

We both stumbled. "What's going on?" I asked.

"It's empty," Sidney said.

I walked in and my breath caught. "Where is everyone?"

"I don't know. There's always a bunch of kids here at any given time." Sidney checked the couches while I looked around each of the games for kids who might be hiding.

"Let's check the arboretum. Maybe someone is in there?" I suggested.

Sidney nodded and led the way. Neither of us spoke as we walked down the hall.

A sweet and sour stench made me plug my nose. It smelled like old garbage that had sat out in the sun for a week with a faint hint of sour peppermint.

Pools of brown surrounded the ice cream trees. Instead of freezer cold air, the hot and muggy air had melted the ice cream.

As we walked on, we passed the pizza bagel bushes. The ground was a mess with rancid cheese and pepperoni. The licorice grass had wilted. Nothing looked as vibrant or pretty as it had before.

Sidney opened up a candy watermelon and gasped. The insides were brown and mushy.

"Everything is rotting or dying," I said, holding my nose.

Sidney dropped the watermelon. "What's happening?"

We stood next to each other, surveying the area in the silence. Sidney slipped her hand in mine and I squeezed it.

"I don't know. We need to figure this out, though."

A rustling noise to the left made us both jump. Sidney let go and turned toward the source.

"Is anyone there?" Sidney called.

Lauren stepped out from behind a tree. Her clothes were stained and tattered. Leaves and twigs stuck out of her tangled hair. "Sidney? Oh, my goodness, I'm glad to see you!" She ran up to Sidney and pulled her into a hug.

"What happened to you?" Sidney asked.

Lauren stepped back. "I was looking for Rafa. I haven't seen him for days. This place was empty and freaked me out." Lauren brushed the hair out of her wide eyes. "I thought maybe he'd be in the cloud maze but I can't get there. With how bad the storm is, I don't even know if the maze is still in the sky." She gestured toward the sky. "I ended up landing in the forest." She paused and grabbed Sidney's arm. "I saw a man in the forest, and I think he had one of the kids with him."

"Like, an adult?" Sidney asked.

"Yeah, an adult." Lauren dropped Sidney's arm.

"Is that not normal?" I hadn't thought about how there weren't adults here.

Lauren shook her head. "This whole island is for kids. Adults have their own place."

"I've been there once. I used to explore everything I could, on or off the island." Sidney shook her head. "Their island isn't bad or scary or anything."

Lauren flickered. "Oh, no. I think I'm waking up." She

grabbed Sidney's arm again. "Keep looking for Rafa. I'm worried about him. He's never gone missing before."

"We'll keep looking," Sidney told Lauren. Then Lauren winked out.

We spent the rest of the night searching the hideout but couldn't find him anywhere. We did find a room full of old dolls —some looked a hundred years old. The shelves also held jacks and marbles; hoops and sticks; and several old jars filled with an assortment of candy.

Eventually Sidney started flickering. "I think my mom is waking me up. Text me when you can."

She disappeared and I was left alone.

Chapter
14

At the hospital the next morning, workers bustled about the halls, all walking with a purpose. We walked straight to the radiology department and checked in. I sat between Mom and Dad in the aquarium room again. Dad scratched my back and Mom kept her hand on my knee. Their touch comforted me today.

"Why am I getting this test?" I asked Mom. "What's the difference between this one and the one from yesterday?" My stomach growled. I had to fast again.

"The doctor said they use both tests to see what's happening in your body. The PET scan from yesterday will show the cancer and how your organs are functioning, but it doesn't give a clear picture of your organs." Mom shifted in her seat to look at me better. "The CT scan will give a clear picture of your organs but doesn't show how they are functioning. If they look at both images, they're able to see where the cancer is."

"Jessa?" A nurse stood at the door holding two bottles and a clipboard. "Follow me." We stood and followed the nurse to another waiting room.

Several kids sat with their parents. A little girl around Kate's age cried while her mom held a cup and whispered in her ear. A teenaged boy sat across the room holding a bottle. His head was leaned against the wall and his eyes were closed. Another small girl had curled up on a couch with her thumb in her mouth and her eyes glued to the movie playing on the TV.

"For the CT scan you'll have to drink this contrast." The nurse shook one of the bottles. "Once you've finished, we have to wait about an hour before we can start the scan." She held out both bottles—they were about the size of a large bottle of soda. "Would you like piña colada or banana? It's like a smoothie."

I shrugged. "Which one tastes better?" A smoothie didn't sound too bad.

"I think most people prefer piña colada." She handed one of the bottles to me. "Neither is very tasty, though." She pulled a straw out of her pocket and handed it to me as well. "You need to drink the whole thing. Here are some tips: don't smell it, and try not to let it touch your tongue—so either chug it or sip it through a straw."

I didn't know how to respond. This sounded less good.

The nurse pulled something from the wall and handed it to Mom. "Just in case it comes back up." A blue rubbery round ring sat atop a long blue tube made of grocery bag material. "If she does vomit, you can twist the bag like this, tie it off, and throw it away." She demonstrated what to do, then handed it back to Mom. "Take as many as you need."

"Thanks," Mom said.

"We'd like her to drink as much as she can, but if she makes it to here"—the nurse drew a line on the bottle at the half-way mark—"that should be enough. The more we can get inside of her, the better the picture will be."

Anxiety bloomed inside my chest. Was the contrast that bad? Dad led us to an open couch and we sat down. He took the drink from me and unscrewed the top. A layer of foil covered the opening. Dad took the straw and punctured the foil enough for the straw to fit through. He handed it back to me. "Cheers."

The first sip wasn't too bad. The overly strong piña colada flavoring didn't mask the chalky medicine flavor. I took several long sips, trying to keep it down before I needed to stop and take a breath. I was fine...until the aftertaste hit me.

I had never experienced anything like it before. Like they'd taken water that had been left in a vase for over a week and mixed it with chalk and vomit, then threw a little piña colada flavoring in. I gagged. The teenage boy looked over at me. What if I puked in front of everyone?

Mom held the puke bag for me. Nothing came out but my confidence waned.

"You can do this, Jessa," Dad said as he pulled my hair out of my face and held it back for me. "You're a strong girl. A strongirl? A strogirl?" he asked.

I tried to take slow breaths. "Both bad options," I croaked.

"She's right," Mom agreed.

Dad grinned. "Are you ready for another sip?"

Mom held the drink out to me.

I nodded and took another sip. My stomach turned at the liquefied chalk. The piña colada "smoothie" tried to escape, but I managed to hold it down.

A boy about my age, sitting across the waiting room from me, puked into his bag. The noise made me shudder.

Palms sweating, I took the drink. I could do this.

I pulled the straw out and opened the foil the rest of the way. Plugging my nose, I took a big gulp. As soon as my mouth filled with the foul liquid, I regretted it. The chalky taste and the texture together pushed me over the edge. My stomach revolted and I grabbed the puke bag and vomited.

Dad held my hair for me. "It's okay, Jessa. It's okay," he murmured.

Mom handed me a Styrofoam cup of tepid water.

I swished the metallic tasting water then spat it into the puke bag. Mom tied the bag off and took it across the room to the garbage.

"I can't do this." A familiar pain prickled behind my eyes. Dad pulled me into a hug and I started to cry.

"I know, kiddo." He held my head up against his. "I'm sorry you have to go through this."

"It's not fair." I pulled away to look at Dad. My hair stuck to his scruffy face, making me feel like I'd just played with a balloon. He brushed the hair off.

Dad held me by the shoulders and looked me right in the eyes. "You're right, it's not fair. You're too young to have to go through this. But, honey, this is what's happening. If you don't drink this contrast, they're not going to get the best picture of what's going on inside your body." He let go of my shoulders and held both of my hands in his. "We have to get the whole picture if we want to smash this cancer. You are a strong girl. I know you can do this."

I looked away from his hopeful eyes, letting the tears roll down my cheeks. "I'm not strong," I whispered. My face burned with shame.

Dad scooped me into his lap and pushed my head onto his shoulder. His scruffy whiskers poked my forehead. He sighed. "Jessa, if you could see yourself through my eyes. You *are* strong. You're amazing and talented. You're beautiful and brave. You do anything you put your mind to." He gave me a tight squeeze. "*You* need to believe all those things—see yourself how I see you."

More tears rolled down my cheeks and I sniffed. "I'm not those things—I'm not brave," I mumbled. Then, the words spilled out before I could stop them. "I'm scared."

"Oh, honey. Being brave doesn't mean you aren't afraid— just the opposite. Courage comes *when* you're scared and you face your fears anyway." Leaning away, he put his finger under my chin and lifted my face to look at him. His calloused finger scratched my skin. "Here's a secret: most people don't feel strong. Most people feel weak and inadequate. The trick is to pretend you're strong. That's it. You pretend you're strong and you'll *be* strong." His rough hands gently wiped my tears away.

I closed my eyes and sighed. Could it be that simple?

Mom walked over with a small paper cup and another puke bag. "The nurse suggested we pour a little in the cup and work on one cupful at a time."

Dad pulled me in for another hug. "Are you ready to try again?" he murmured into my hair.

I shook my head.

He pushed me away to see me better. "Say this: I'm brave. I'm strong. I can do hard things."

I shook my head.

"Say it," Dad said, with a smile.

I knew where this would go. Dad wouldn't stop until I'd said it. I took a breath and muttered, "I'm brave, I'm strong, I can do hard things."

"Jess, say it with confidence." He scooted me back onto my chair and said it louder. "I'm brave. I'm strong. I can do hard things."

A few of the other patients and their parents looked over at us. My face burned. "Dad, everyone is looking at us."

He lowered his voice. "That's okay. Let them look. Maybe we can help them, too. Maybe one of them needs to hear these words. But I think it'll mean more coming from you." He smiled at me. "Now, say it like you mean it."

I sighed. "I'm brave, I'm strong, I can do hard things."

"I don't believe you," Dad said in a mocking tone. "Convince me."

Did I feel brave? Was Dad right about courage? The idea that I was allowed to be scared made me feel like a weight had been lifted from my shoulders. Being strong and brave meant I just had to keep going. Maybe I could do this, even if I felt scared.

I stood up—a couple of the kids looked at me. I ignored them and, injecting all the fake confidence I could muster, said, "I'm brave. I'm strong. I can do hard things." And I felt it. The fear still existed, but it wasn't holding me hostage anymore. I felt like I'd shrugged off a wet blanket.

Mom handed me the little paper cup, half full of the contrast, and I downed the contents in one gulp.

"That's my girl!" Dad's smile could have brightened the sun. "You're brave. You're strong. You can do hard things."

Mom poured another cup and I swallowed it easily.

The contrast still made me feel nauseous but I pushed past it and drank another little cup. When it was too overpowering, we took a short break. But sooner than I expected, the bottle was empty.

Dad cheered and kissed my forehead. Mom handed me a piece of hard candy to get the flavor out of my mouth. Another kid's mom clapped for me. I stole a glance at the teenage boy. His bottle was empty too. We locked eyes and he gave me a small nod and smile. I closed my eyes and concentrated on the words Dad had put in my mind.

I was strong.

I was brave.

I could do hard things.

FOR THE NEXT week during school, the teachers seemed extra nice to me, along with most of the kids. Everyone knew. News like this spread like wildfire at school. Michael showed up at my locker between each class to help me open it. Carleigh and

Anna treated me about the same: warm one minute and cold the next. Alexa spent most of her time with Carleigh. I caught her glancing at me during class and at lunch, but she didn't say much to me.

How could I be in the spotlight but still be alone?

A week after my scans, Mom and Dad asked me to come into their room to talk. Mom patted a spot on her bed. I sank into the puffy white comforter. Dad knelt down next to me.

I could feel the seriousness of the conversation from the expressions on their faces. Mom sniffed and held a tissue up to her nose. I never thought I'd be the reason Mom cried so much. I focused on Dad. I couldn't look at Mom while she was in so much pain because of me.

"The doctor called with your scan results." Dad put his hand on my knee.

My heart rate tripled.

"You have Hodgkin lymphoma stage 2B."

"What does that mean?" I whispered.

Dad squeezed my knee. "Your scan showed you have another tumor. Stage 2 cancer means you have tumors in more than one place."

Another tumor. My stomach turned. I tried to slow my breathing but I couldn't. I felt on the edge of control but I was slipping fast.

"They found a tumor between your lungs," Dad continued.

"Do I need surgery again?" My skin tingled at the thought.

"The tumor is in a tricky spot. The doctors said the best way to get rid of it is to shrink it through chemotherapy and radiation. You'll have eight weeks of chemo and then, assuming your scans look good, two weeks of radiation." Dad pulled me into a brief hug. "The good news is we caught it pretty early. The tumor is about the size of an orange."

Mom sniffed. Tears fell from her red-rimmed eyes.

"What does the B mean?" I asked.

"The B means you've had symptoms—night sweats, weight loss, no appetite." Dad took my hands and looked me in the eyes. "They said this is very treatable. Your outcome is really good. They want to start on chemotherapy next week. After a few rounds of chemo, they'll do more scans and take a look at the tumor again."

I didn't know what to say, but the words came out on their own. "Outcome? Chemo? Treatable?" My voice started as a whisper but rose as I spoke. "Are these words supposed to make me feel better? You're saying all of this like it's good news." I was shouting at Dad —almost crying. "I. Have. Cancer. That's not good!"

I pulled my hands out of his and stormed out of their room, slamming my door when I had retreated to the safety of my room. The tears streamed down my cheeks. I threw myself face first onto my bed.

A few minutes later, Mom knocked and cracked the door open. "Jessa?"

"Go away!" I yelled. I didn't want to see anyone. I didn't want to talk about how cancer was such "good news."

The door shut.

I rolled onto my side expecting to see Mom standing there, but the room was empty.

Great. Mom and Dad were trying to be nice. I shouldn't have exploded at them. It wasn't their fault. My throat felt thick and my stomach hurt.

The door opened again, and Sarah came in. She didn't say anything as she walked over and sat on my bed. I rolled away from her.

Tears pooled on the side of my nose until they fell onto my pillow.

Sarah curled up behind me and put her arm around me,

pulling me into her chest. I cried harder, and behind me, Sarah cried with me.

THE TREE HOUSE swayed back and forth in the harsh wind.

"Did you find Rafa?" I asked.

"No, I can't find anyone. Not even Lauren." Sidney said. We walked to the doorway. "We need to figure this out."

The sky was overcast, the waves crashed louder and harder, and the wind whipped through the trees.

We slid down the fireman's pole. Neither of us dared fly from this height; the wind might blow us away.

"Where should we look?" I asked.

"I've been thinking about it, and I have an idea," Sidney said with a frown. "I've been there once, a long time ago: Skull Island. It's on the other side of the mountain, though."

"Sounds suspicious," I joked. "Lead the way."

We tried to fly low to the ground, but the wind was pushing us back just as hard as we were flying forward. We didn't move; we just floated in the same spot, fighting the wind until we both landed, exhausted.

"I don't think we can fly in this wind," Sidney said, panting from her effort.

"Agreed," I said, just as breathless. "Looks like we'll be walking around the island."

We started walking toward the mountain; the wind pushed us back like a giant invisible hand. The plants looked burned and rotting like we'd seen up in the tree house. One tree lay on the ground, knocked over by the wind. The inside of the tree had leaked out and a puddle of black goo, smelling of overly sweet peppermint, lay at the base.

We didn't speak much as we hiked around the mountain to the far side of the island where found refuge in a small cave.

We both collapsed, safe from the elements. I crawled to one of the walls and sat against it.

Sidney yawned, crawling over to sit next to me. "I'm so tired. That wind was exhausting."

"Can you sleep in Dreamland?" I asked.

"I've never tried," Sidney said, then a little softer, "I've never wanted to." She twisted her bracelet around on her wrist.

"Your bracelet looks different. Did you add more beads?" I asked.

"I like to change it up."

I held my arm up for her to see mine. "It's small."

"For now." Sidney slipped her bracelet off and held it out to me.

I took it from her and examined it. Several big beads separated the smaller beads.

"Which are your favorites?" I asked.

"This one," she indicated the bead in the middle, "I chose it after my first clear scan when I was six."

By far the biggest bead, it was a yellow square with an 'S' on it, surrounded by little rays.

"It reminds me of the sun," I said.

"Me too." Sidney smiled.

"What about this one?" I pointed to a chunky, wooden circle.

"I got that after a surgery, I think."

"And this one?" I fingered a black metal star.

"ICU for several weeks—not a fun time. I've never seen another bead like it, though." Sidney pointed to the smaller beads. "These regular beads are for things like a chemo treatment or a CT scan. The glow-in-the-dark beads are given after radiation."

"Why is it so loose?" I could slide the beads around easily. "Are you missing one?"

Sidney put her head on my shoulder. "I'm saving that spot for when I'm done with cancer."

"These are really cool. Maybe you can show me how to make a better bracelet when I get more beads." I said.

"I'd love to," Sidney replied. She cocked her head to one side. "Do you hear that?"

I strained to hear anything. The eerie silence brought goosebumps to my arms.

I shivered. "What?" I whispered.

"The wind has stopped." She jumped up and headed outside. I followed close on her heels.

The black clouds still looked menacing, but the air was still.

I rose from the ground and held my hand out to Sidney. "Let's go while we can!"

We soared up until we were right above the trees.

The island streaked below us in a green and brown blur as we flew over it.

"Have you explored past the mountain?" I asked.

"Yeah, but the hideout and my meadow are my favorite places," she replied. "This way." She pulled my hand and we flew faster toward the tip of the island.

A drop of rain hit my face and lightning struck in the distance.

"We need to go back to the ground," I said. "The lightning could be dangerous."

"Just a little farther."

The wind picked up, blowing us off course. More raindrops pelted me. Sid led us out over the open ocean. Thunder boomed in the distance and the waves crashed wildly below.

"How much farther?" My heart pounded inside my chest like it wanted to escape.

"It's coming." She pointed to a gray mass in the distance. "There."

I almost couldn't distinguish it from the ocean, but when I looked carefully, I could see another island.

The wind blew harder as we fought our way closer to it. When it came into view, I recoiled. A giant skull as tall as the waterfall smiled up at me. Dead vines covered the top like giant worms.

"I think we found Skull Island," I ventured.

Sidney pulled me forward until we could land on top of the giant head. "This place freaks me out."

We moved around the top, trying not to slip in the rain. I stood atop the skull, looking down at the eye holes below me. Sidney stepped up next to me and squeezed my hand. We had to go in. The rain poured down on us as we both jumped off the edge. I twisted in time to see the sightless eyes staring at me.

Sidney pulled me into one of the sockets and we both landed lightly on the edge. Below us lay a hallway. I recognized the old, stained carpet. "I don't believe it." I never expected to see my school in Dreamland.

"Where are we? Do you know it?" Sidney asked softly as we tiptoed past the rows of lockers.

"Yeah, this is my school," I whispered. "We're in one of the sixth-grade halls. My locker is down the other hall." We came to the end and peeked into the main hall. It looked exactly like school. We were down by Miss Chi's class. "My homeroom is right there." I pointed to the last door at the end of the hall.

"Why are we at the school?" Sidney asked.

Just then we heard a man's voice shouting down by the common area. "What are you doing out of class?"

Sidney and I both jumped. She grabbed my hand and pulled me through the nearest door, which was the girls' bathroom. We kept the door cracked open so we could hear.

"I...I don't know," said a girl. "Where am I? How'd I get here?" Her voice sounded familiar.

I glanced at Sidney. "Is that Lauren?" I whispered.

Sidney squeezed my hand. I looked over and she put her finger to her lips. "Shh," she breathed.

"You're at school," the man said, "and you're in the halls without a hall pass. That means detention."

"What? Let me go!" the girl shouted.

I couldn't take it anymore. I slipped out of the bathroom and peeked around the corner into the main hall. I could see all the way down to the common area. The man held Lauren by the arm and dragged her into one of my classrooms.

I recognized him and froze in place.

"You'll stay in detention until you've learned your lesson." Mr. Black opened the classroom door and we got a quick view of the inside. Kids sat at the desks, all working.

The door closed and silence fell in the hall.

"It's Mr. Black. Did you see him?" I whispered. Why was he here?

"He has Lauren," Sidney said under her breath. "Did you see all the kids in there?"

"We need to get out of here before he comes back. We know where everyone is now. Maybe we can come up with a plan." I gave Sidney's hand a gentle tug, and we made our way back up the hall into the shadows we'd hid in earlier. The skull eyes were out of reach.

"It's too high," I said, focusing on a happy thought so we could fly back up. I thought of Kate and my family. But nothing happened. I thought of the observatory but my feet stayed firmly on the ground. Nothing worked.

I turned to Sidney. "I can't fly."

She hovered a few inches off the floor. "This is as high as I can go." Her panic-filled expression made my palms sweat.

A door shut in the main hall behind us.

"Did you hear that?" I whispered.

"He's coming. We have to get out of here." Sidney grabbed my hand.

I concentrated hard on flying. My feet lifted off the ground. "We must be stronger together." I squeezed Sidney's hand and we flew out the eye socket.

The wind blew hard, but as long as we held hands and flew together, it didn't affect us.

Lightning struck nearby. My hand faded.

I could feel myself roll over in my bed in the real world even as the rain pounded down on me in Dreamland.

Sidney squeezed my hand harder and I returned to Dreamland.

We hovered low above the crashing waves. Sidney continued forward, pulling me with her.

"I'm waking up!" I shouted to Sidney.

She didn't answer but increased our speed.

We could only fly together in the storm. What would happen to Sidney if I faded and she didn't? She needed me to fly with her. She couldn't do it alone. I focused all my energy on the sandy beach.

I could feel myself fading again. It was like being in two places at the same time. I could feel my body, hot and sweaty, under my covers and the cool breeze of the fan on my face. But I could also feel the wind pushing me and hear the undulating ocean beneath me.

A wave smashed into us.

"We're too close to the water!" Sidney shouted. She pulled my arm and helped me fly higher. We rapidly approached the beach.

I could hear my clock. Tick tock. Tick tock.

We landed hard in the sand. Sidney pulled on my arm and helped me up. "Let's go."

I opened my eyes. My bed was soaked in sweat.

Chapter
15

A week later we were back at the hospital for my first chemotherapy treatment. Mom walked to the information desk. "Oncology?"

"Third floor," the man said.

I turned toward Dad. "Oncology means cancer?"

"Yes." Dad led us to the elevator bays, and we rode to the third floor.

My chest tightened and my palms started sweating. What was going to happen today? It was my first chemo treatment. I had wanted to talk to Sidney this last week, but she'd been too sick to respond to my texts, and I couldn't find her in Dreamland. I hoped she hadn't been captured. We had to figure out what to do and why Mr. Black was putting kids in detention. I couldn't fly in the strong wind alone to check Skull Island—I needed Sidney.

Dad took my hand and we walked down the hall together. The bright colors gave the hallway a cheery feeling. Framed, hand-drawn pictures hung on walls every few feet. A hand-drawn map caught my eye. A big mountain sat in the middle. On the right, tiny palm trees dotted the sandy beaches. Off to the left a river ran through a forest. I touched a small tan square in the middle of the forest where the tree house sat. I traced the river with my finger down to the waterfall. Dreamland.

"Pretty pictures." Dad admired the map with me. He leaned

forward to get a closer look. "Wow, this kid was only seven. Are those mazes drawn into the clouds? I've never seen that before."

I thought of flying through the cloud maze and smiled. "Rafa," I whispered.

"What?" Dad pointed to the plaque under the frame. "This says, 'Lauren, age seven.'"

Lauren? I took a closer look at the picture. If I hadn't known what to look for, I wouldn't have seen it. Mermaids, all with colorful hair, were sunning themselves on the rocks around the lagoon.

"C'mon, Jess," Mom called from down the hall. She stood under a bright green *Oncology* sign.

Still holding Dad's hand, I took a few steps toward Mom, but stopped when I noticed Dad wasn't moving. I looked back at him. He was still studying the map, one finger touching the entrance to the hideout. "Dad, we've got to go." I pulled on his hand again.

Dad turned away from the map and together we walked through double doors into the lobby of the oncology ward.

Several bald kids sat in the waiting room, most wearing masks. A girl about my age sat wrapped up in a blanket. A few tufts of dark brown hair stuck out the bottom of her crocheted beanie. Wires for her earbuds ran down from her ears and into her pocket. Eyes squeezed and jaw clenched tight, she seemed to be in pain.

Would that be me in a few months?

A crowd of workers surrounded one little boy. One of the workers was reading a poem on the wall. Everyone was smiling at him. His mom rubbed his bald head, and he smiled up at her. She walked him over to a bell where he grabbed a golden rope hanging from it and rang the bell three times. Everyone cheered.

"What's going on?" I asked.

Mom shrugged. As the crowd dispersed, we approached to get a better look.

The golden bell was fastened to the wall. The silky, golden rope hung down from it. Next to it was a plaque with a gold background and black lettering. It said

> *Ring this bell three times well*
> *A toll will clearly say,*
> *"My treatment is done*
> *This course is run*
> *And I am on my way!"*

J. L. Kennington

"He must be done with his treatments," Mom said. She wrapped me in a one-armed hug. "You'll be ringing it in a few months."

Dad squeezed my hand. "You're strong, right?"

I shrugged and sat down. Dad handed me his phone. Before I could get into my game, the nurse called my name. My stomach tightened. I stood up and walked over to the nurse.

She looked at Mom. "We need to do her PICC line first, so come back here with me."

We followed her into a sterile, white room. A paper covered table sat in the middle of the room. A tray with instruments on it sat next to the table. The nurse wore a mask and a blue paper gown. "What's a PICC line?" I asked. I sat down on the table.

"It's a special tube we leave in your arm to give you medicine or other fluids." The nurse donned her gloves. Three other people walked in and started putting on their gowns and masks. "That way we don't have to poke your arm every time you need a treatment or blood draw."

"Does it hurt?" My chest felt tight and hollow at the same

time. I thought about the blood draws and IVs I'd received. Some weren't too bad, but some hurt a lot.

The nurse leaned down to be at eye level with me. Her mask covered her mouth and nose, and her surgical hat sat in the middle of her forehead. I could only see her eyes and eyebrows. "I'm going to be honest. I don't lie to anyone—especially kids. Sometimes putting a PICC line in is easy, and sometimes it's trickier. It almost always hurts when we put the needle in. It feels like a sharp pinch, but after that it usually goes smoothly." She reached out and touched my arm with warm hands. "I've been doing this for over twenty years, so I've done a lot of these."

My chest loosened a bit, and I nodded.

I lay down on the table, and they put a blue drape over the whole bed. I turned my head away and looked at Mom and Dad. A worker explained what would happen to me as they used a machine to look for a good vein in the upper part of my right arm. I felt like I had a hundred of Sidney's butterflies inside me.

As they did the procedure, the worker let me watch a movie on a tablet. Mom and Dad helped me hold still and kept me calm, though I could only see them through watery eyes. At one point they asked me to turn my head down toward the arm they were putting it in. It didn't feel very good but, soon it was over.

When they removed the drape, I could see a thin, clear dressing on my arm, covering up the tube. They covered the whole thing with a stretchy pink sleeve. The nurse walked us back to the waiting room. "We drew some blood and when the results come back, they'll call you back again for your treatment."

What would chemo feel like? Would it be cold? Or maybe burn? I had heard somewhere that chemo was poison. I shuddered. I knew why I needed it, but it didn't change the fact they would be putting poison in my body on purpose.

After a long time, but still too soon, the nurse called my name again. I felt jumpy. I wanted to get chemo over with, but I also didn't want to do it at all.

The nurses gave me a choice of a game console, a tablet, or a movie to watch. I picked the tablet and started playing a game while they unwrapped my arm to access my PICC line. They shot fluid up the line.

"This is saline. It's a special mix of fluids to help keep you hydrated. It's sort of like drinking water." The nurse hooked up a big tube to my PICC line, then stood and adjusted something farther up the line. Another nurse hung a red bag of fluid alongside the saline. They both checked it and wrote something on the bag, then the other nurse left. The nurse hooked it up to my clear tube, and the red liquid flowed down the line and into my arm.

A few seconds later, a strange metallic taste came into my mouth. I scrunched my nose.

"You taste that?" The nurse handed me a cup of juice.

"Yeah." I took a sip.

"That's the chemo." She pulled a wrapped yellow candy from her pocket and held it out to me. "Here. They say eating something sour helps. I always keep a few of these in my pocket."

I took it and popped it into my mouth. The lemon candy made my lips pucker. The nurse laughed and handed me a few more. "Let me know if you run out." She winked and turned to talk to Mom.

Cold flooded into my arm and crawled its way up from the PICC line into my chest. The hairs on my right arm stood straight up. My left arm wasn't cold, but I shivered anyway.

A worker came into the room with a few blankets. She set them down on the foot of the bed and started spreading them over me. The warmth enveloped me like a big hug or a warm bath.

I tried not to think about the fluid as it dripped into me. Poison. They were giving me *poison*. On purpose.

I played on the tablet but my thoughts strayed to Sidney. Was she at the hospital? Was she in Dreamland? Had she been scared with every treatment, or had they become normal after a while?

The treatment finished, and they gave me extra fluids to help keep me hydrated. They let me pick out a bead to add to my collection. The doctor gave Mom a prescription for more medicine, and we were on our way home.

"How are you feeling?" Dad asked as we walked to the car. The sun sat low in the sky. We'd spent most of the day at the hospital.

"I'm okay, I think." I expected to feel more poisoned, but I didn't feel much different, just tired. "Can I text Alexa, Mom?"

"Texlexa?" Dad asked.

I smiled. "I don't think so, Dad." I hadn't thought to text her earlier. I'd been too nervous. She had been acting weird at school since the night she and Mrs. Johnston had come over. Maybe she didn't know how to act around me now, like when Sidney was first diagnosed and I didn't know what to say to her. But maybe if I could show her that *I* hadn't changed it wouldn't be weird. She'd realize I was still the same person she'd been friends with for years. I missed my best friend.

We got in the car and Mom handed her phone back to me.

I pulled up the text app and found Alexa.

Hey, how's it going?

I held the phone, waiting for Alexa to respond.

Fine. How's hospital life? Alexa replied.

I sighed in relief. She'd responded. Maybe things could go back to normal. **It's okay, just finished my first**

treatment. I stared at the screen for a moment before typing. **Want to come over tonight or tomorrow?**

I waited for her text but the phone never buzzed. Maybe she was busy. We stopped at the pharmacy but I stayed in the car while Mom and Dad went in. My eyes burned. I wanted to lie down. My skin started to hurt. I pulled a blanket over myself and shivered.

We stopped at a fast food restaurant and Dad bought me chicken nuggets and fries. The food smelled okay but everything tasted metallic and gross.

Alexa still hadn't texted back by the time we left the city. On a whim I texted Sidney's Mom.

This is Jessa. Can you give this message to Sidney? I finished my first chemo treatment. How are you doing?

The phone buzzed in my hand a moment later. Alexa? No —Sidney.

This is Sidney. How'd it go? Did you get sick? I almost always do.

No. It was better than I thought. Better than the CT scan anyway. I popped a fry in my mouth and spat it back out.

The contrast is the worst! I have to do one next week. :(Glad you didn't get sick. Watch out for the next few days, though. You might throw up, get a fever, or mouth sores. I'm always exhausted after. I feel like I sleep the whole week in between treatments.

I rubbed my eyes. **I'm already tired. I just want to sleep.**

Meet me in Dreamland! We can hang out there.

I'll try. I handed the phone back to Mom. Thankfully we'd brought my pillow. I propped it against the window and before I knew it, I was asleep.

A TORRENT of wind made the tree house sway and creak. My stomach growled. I had only choked down one nugget and a few fries.

Sidney appeared next to me. "Jessa!" she squealed and pulled me into a quick hug. "How are you feeling?"

"Here? I'm feeling fantastic." I wasn't tired. I didn't have the funny taste in my mouth.

"I know. I love this place." Sidney grinned for a moment then her smile slipped and she looked at the floor. "In real life I'm asleep in a hospital bed. I have so many mouth sores, and I've lost too much weight, they had to put a tube in my nose to feed me."

"That sounds awful. I'm really sorry." I put my arm around her. "I wish I could have visited you."

"I haven't been awake much." Sidney said. "This is better."

"I'm asleep in the car. I couldn't eat much food. Nothing sounded good, and everything tasted weird." I gasped with a realization. "Let's go to the arboretum. We can eat pizza bagels and ice cream and candy." I grabbed her hand and stepped toward the door. Rain poured down flying diagonally in the wind. My heart sank. "I forgot the arboretum was full of rotting food last time." My shoulders fell.

Sidney closed her eyes and scrunched her face up in concentration. Glass appeared on all the windows while a door appeared on the tree house entrance. Sidney reached out and pulled it shut silencing the wind. A few of the hammocks disappeared to make room for two tables. In one corner sat a table stacked with games. The other table sat in the opposite corner and had food piled on it—hot dogs, pizza, crackers, apples with caramel dip, and a lot of candy.

My mouth hung open. I closed it with a snap. "How did you do that?"

Sidney smiled. "I thought really hard about what I wanted this room to look like. You can do it too."

"I dunno. I can barely dry my clothes after the waterfall. And I still can't change my appearance." I held up my arm, showing off the pink sleeve where my new PICC line had been placed.

Sidney flashed a smile, and a purple sleeve appeared on her arm—same place as mine. "Give it a try. Is there something you want that I forgot about?" she asked.

I walked over to the table and looked through the food on it. "I like those powdered, raspberry-filled donuts."

Sidney's eyes sparkled. "Me too. Think of a full package sitting on the table."

I closed my eyes and imagined the table exactly how it looked now, then I added the box of white donuts. I could see it, right there, between the pizza and the licorice. Sidney gasped and I opened my eyes.

The box of donuts sat right where I'd pictured it. As I reached for it, it flickered and disappeared.

"Good try." Sidney screwed up her face again and the donuts appeared and stayed. She opened her eyes, grabbed the box, and handed it to me. "It takes practice. Here you go."

I opened the box and sunk my teeth into the soft pastry.

Sidney sat down at the table and took a donut.

"Why do you think Mr. Black is keeping our friends at the school?" Sidney asked, taking a bite of her donut. "And what is he even doing here?"

"It sounded like he thinks he's actually at Sunnyside.

Remember how he was asking Lauren for a hall pass?" I took another bite of my donut and jelly dripped out of the middle and onto the table. "He put her in detention."

"Okay," Sidney said, licking the powdered sugar off of her fingers. "But why is he even here? Adults don't come here."

"A boy at school told me Mr. Black is still really sad because his wife died. He's in the hospital getting help. Maybe that's why." I wiped the powdered sugar from my mouth. "Do you think Dreamland created the school inside the island as his gift? Or could he have created it, like you made all this food?" I indicated the pile of mostly untouched food on the table.

"I don't think Dreamland would give him a school. He probably doesn't realize he's dreaming and projected it," Sidney said.

"It's almost like Rafa's ghost stories," I suggested. "A dark version of something that hurts the other kids."

"But school's not a bad thing," Sydney objected.

"A school you can never leave is," I said.

Sidney groaned and covered her face. "Why didn't I think about Rafa's stories before?" she asked through her hands.

"Because you thought it was just a legend," I reassured her. "Don't feel bad for not believing in old ghost stories."

She set her hands in her lap but was still shaking her head. "Do you think the school is the reason Dreamland is dying?"

"Maybe. Do the stories ever say how to fix it?" I picked up a piece of pizza and took a bite.

"I don't know." Sidney sighed. She pulled the pizza box over but didn't pick up a slice. "So, if Mr. Black thinks he's teaching school, maybe we could trick him into thinking school is out."

"And he'd let the kids out of detention." I smiled. "Good idea."

"Then maybe he'd leave Dreamland and everything would

go back to normal." Sidney finally picked up a slice of pizza and took a big bite.

"So how do we trick him?" I asked.

Sidney frowned. "I don't know."

I woke up when we pulled into the driveway. Dreamland had been wonderful but I wished the effects carried over. Why couldn't I stay there, where I felt awake and free? As soon as I awoke, everything Dreamland had masked came back to me. I was nauseated, exhausted even though I'd just slept, and shivering with chills. *Now* I felt poisoned.

I walked straight to the couch and collapsed into it, too tired to even go upstairs. I texted Alexa again while I lay on the couch. **I just got home. Want to hang out tomorrow?** My body felt drained, but it would be nice to see her.

Mom unpacked the car. She lined a bunch of medicines up on the counter along with a box of masks I had to wear around any visitors.

Sarah came and sat down next to me. She hadn't been her usual, snotty self, which was a nice change. She scooped my head into her lap and started braiding my hair.

My hair that would soon fall out. I was going to be bald.

The stark difference between how my body felt ten minutes ago in Dreamland and how it felt now hit me even harder. My world was crashing down on me. A tear leaked out of my eye.

Sarah leaned down and kissed my head. "I'm so sorry, Jessa."

Kate sat down on the ground and leaned her back against the couch. "I painted you a picture." She held up a piece of paper with a butterfly, carefully painted to cover the whole paper. She'd colored one wing blue and one rainbow. It reminded me of Sidney's butterfly meadow.

"Thanks, Kate. It's beautiful." I sniffed.

Mom turned on a movie. Dad put a blanket over the top of me then settled onto the other sofa next to Mom with a bag of popcorn. Kate went to snuggle between them.

I struggled to keep my heavy eyelids open. I shivered under the fuzzy blanket. Sarah pressed her cool hand to my forehead. The smell of popcorn made my stomach churn.

Mom's phone buzzed in my hand. Alexa?

No, just *abuela* asking Mom how my treatment went. I didn't want to see what they said about me. I was going to be the subject of all the gossip for a while.

I texted Sidney again. **Just got home. Hope you're doing okay.**

The doorbell rang and Mom left to answer it.

"Hi, Mrs. Newberry," a boy's voice said.

I tuned out the conversation and focused on the movie. I was surprised when Mom bent down in front of me.

"You have a friend from school who wants to say hi. Do you think you're up for it?" Mom's eyebrows were drawn together in obvious concern.

"Who is it?" I asked. I couldn't think of a boy from school who would visit me.

"He said his name was Michael?" She said it as a question. "Do you know him? Curly dark hair and a cute smile?"

"Yeah, I know him."

"Can I tell him he can come in?" Mom asked.

Why would Michael come without being invited but Alexa wouldn't even answer my text? "I don't want to see anyone right now," I lied, trying to keep the frustration out of my voice. I did want to see Alexa or Sidney—not Michael.

Mom kissed my head and went back to the front door.

"He brought you brownies," she said when she returned. "And a cute, little stuffed cat."

I took the stuffed cat and held it to my chest, feeling a little lighter somehow. "You guys eat them. Nothing sounds good to me."

Kate ran to the kitchen and returned with a hand full of paper towels. She passed out the brownies on a paper towel to everyone with Mom's help. She set mine on the floor.

The smell of popcorn and brownies made my stomach turn even more. Bile rose up my throat. I tried to stand up to run to the bathroom, but my legs were tangled in the blanket. I ended up on all fours on the ground, retching. Sarah shoved a garbage under my face and held my hair back.

It burned coming up. I cried as I puked, over and over. I could feel someone rubbing my back. Somebody else put a cool, damp washcloth on the back of my neck.

When it was over, Sarah took the garbage can away and I collapsed onto the floor. Dad picked me up and carried me to my room. He set me on my bed and disappeared for a minute. When he came back, he held my toothbrush, mouthwash, and two cups.

"From what we've read and what the doctor told us, this is normal, sweetie," he said sitting down on my bed. He handed me the toothbrush already loaded with toothpaste. "But that doesn't mean it's not miserable. I'm sorry, baby girl." He only called us baby girl when something was really wrong.

I brushed the bile from my mouth, rinsed with the mouthwash, and spat it all in the empty cup. I took a few sips from the cup with water to get the taste out of my mouth, then lay down.

"There's a garbage right next to your bed in case you start to feel sick again..." He trailed off.

"Thanks, Dad," I mumbled. My eyes drooped.

"Do you want me to stay with you?" he asked.

"Mmm hmm." My pillow cradled my head. A part of me waited for him to crack a joke or combine words together in a lame way. He could almost always cheer me up. But he sat in silence next to me on my bed, stroking my hair as I fell asleep.

Chapter
16

My sleep was fitful. I awoke several times and never went to Dreamland. Dad had fallen asleep on the foot of my bed, his back against the wall, using a couple of my hoodies to stay warm. I threw up once more, and Dad helped me with everything.

Around four in the morning I finally fell into a dreamless sleep. When I woke up, the sun shone through my blinds. The clock read 1:00. I had slept through breakfast and lunch—not that food sounded good at all.

The house felt empty. Sarah and Kate were at school; Dad would be at work. Was Mom home?

I climbed out of bed, still feeling a bit shaky from last night, and padded down the stairs. A note from Mom sat on the counter. She'd gone grocery shopping and wanted me to text her from the kids' phone when I woke up.

My stomach growled. I knew I should eat, but nothing looked good. I settled for a piece of white bread. I nibbled on it as I texted Mom. **I'm up.**

Mom responded almost instantly. **Oh, I was hoping I'd be back before you woke up. Sorry I'm not there, *mijita*. How are you feeling?**

Fine, I typed. **Did I get any messages on your phone?**

Mrs. Thatcher sent something. I'll forward it to

you. The three dots appeared and then the message from Mrs. Thatcher.

Jessa, I'm glad you and Sidney were able to text yesterday. You cheered her up too. I was very sorry to hear about your diagnosis. Please have your mom let me know if we can do anything for you. Sidney has a feeding tube and will be in the hospital for a few weeks at least as we see if she is responding to the latest treatment. Her last scans weren't great, but she's going to have more scans next week. If you're up here for treatments, I know she'd love to see you. Lots of love and healing thoughts.

My heart swelled a little at Mrs. Thatcher's kindness even as my chest tightened. Mrs. Thatcher made it sound like Sidney was getting worse. What if Sidney wasn't okay? In Dreamland she always acted so normal, I often forgot she was sick.

I'm leaving the store. I'll be home in a few. Mom texted me again.

Did Alexa text me? I asked.

I don't see anything from her. I'll see you in a minute, Mom responded.

I crashed on the couch. It seemed softer than normal and before long I was asleep...and awake again in Dreamland.

I WAS ALONE in the tree house when I appeared in Dreamland. For once, the weather seemed normal. The sky was cloudy but calm. And I knew exactly what I wanted to do. I had only been able to visit my observatory once and I really wanted to go back.

Focusing really hard, I was able to make a small chalkboard

appear on the wall of the tree house. I wrote Sidney a quick note with the date included and told her I'd be in the observatory. I didn't want her to wait for me in the tree house when we could be stargazing together.

The journey there was quick, thanks to the good weather. When I arrived, I noticed a long wire starting near my observatory and leading all the way down the north side of the mountain. Otherwise, the clearing looked just as I remembered it.

I breathed a sigh of satisfaction as soon as I hit the Night switch. The room around me faded to twilight, and a beam of night shone on the clouds but didn't show the stars behind them. I lay on the floor and let my body relax as the stars on the walls around me twinkled.

How could we trick Mr. Black? I tried to organize the facts in my mind. He might not realize he was dreaming. He'd accidently created a twisted version of Sunnyside, which might be killing Dreamland. We needed him to think school was out.

I stared at the nighttime cloudy sky. Maybe we could ring the school bell? But I didn't want to go back to school if I could avoid it. And detention didn't have a bell.

And then it hit me. The teachers let kids out of detention after thirty minutes had passed. What if I could make it look like time had passed? I sat up, staring at the telescope. My telescope somehow projected night time. If I pointed it at the island, Mr. Black would see the darkness outside and let the kids out of detention. No teacher would keep their students at school past dark, right?

I stood and turned a knob on the telescope. The dome retracted the rest of the way.

The door opened and Sidney walked in. "Hey, Jessa. I got your note."

"I have an idea about how to trick Mr. Black," I blurted out, and quickly explained my thoughts.

"I like it," Sidney said when I'd finished.

"But, if I tilt the telescope down to Skull Island, then I won't be able to look through the eyepiece because it'll be too high."

"Did you forget you can fly?" Sidney asked.

I laughed. "No, but I don't think I'll be as steady flying as I would be standing."

"Good point." Sidney closed her eyes and scrunched up her nose.

A platform appeared in front of us.

"Smart," I told her.

I flipped the switch back to Day, and together we aimed the telescope toward Skull Island. The platform Sidney had created was sturdy and strong, and I felt safe as I stood on it and looked through the lens. "I've got it," I said after a few minutes of focusing. "Flip the switch."

Sidney turned on the night feature. I focused on the island, trying to make sure the entire island was covered in night.

"What do you see?" Sidney asked. She flew up next to me.

"Just the skull." I held my breath. This had to work. We waited in silence. I kept hoping to see Rafa or Lauren fly out of the skull's eye sockets at any moment.

After several minutes of watching the skull, I looked over at Sidney. "Do you think this will work? Nothing has happened yet."

"Give it a little bit more time," Sidney said. "Did you see the start to the zipline when you flew in?"

"What do you mean?" I asked. "I saw a long wire. Is that the zipline?"

Sidney nodded. "I hear it leads all the way down to the beach. It sounds epic."

I glanced back into the telescope. A large black cloud flew

out from behind the island and started toward us. "Something is coming, but I can't tell what it is. It's blending in too well with the search-night," I said.

"Let me see," Sidney said. I moved over to give her space. "I don't see anything. Oh! There it is." Sidney looked over at me. Her face paled and her wide eyes shone with worry. "I've never seen that before."

"What?" I asked.

"Take a look." She stepped aside, and I looked into the telescope again.

A giant, black pirate ship floated through the clouds, right toward us. "I've seen that ship," I said. "A few times. Is that Mr. Black's ship?"

"Maybe. It's coming from the island. I don't think we tricked him." Sidney flew off the platform and flipped the switch from Night to Day. "Can you see it better now?"

Once the telescope was in day mode, I was able to zoom in on the ship. On the deck, next to a spoked wheel, Mr. Black stared back at me through a spyglass. I jumped back. "It's him."

"We should get out of here. He knows we're here. What if he's coming to put *us* in detention?" Sidney asked.

I joined Sidney on the ground and flipped the switch that would close the observatory roof. My chest felt tight.

"Can you wake yourself up?" Sidney asked.

"I've never done it," I said. My hands were starting to tremble.

"Concentrate really hard on where you fell asleep. Find something to focus on, like your blankets or a clock—something that isn't around us right now."

Closing my eyes, I took a couple of slow, deep breaths. Where had I fallen asleep? My bed—no, the couch. I focused as hard as I could.

I felt the couch beneath me. Was the blanket twisted around my legs?

The fan hummed. Could I feel it?

My heart raced.

Did I just roll over?

I tried to focus on the living room and forget the pirate ship sailing toward us.

I could hear voices. Mom and Dad?

I grabbed on to the thought of my parents' voices and dragged myself into the real world.

Dreamland was gone. I took a few slow breaths. The feeling of urgency still lingered. I pushed the blankets onto the floor. Had Sidney escaped?

I could see my reflection on the TV. I could also see Mom in the kitchen behind me. She was talking to Dad on speaker phone while she cooked. The aroma of cooking veggies reached me and made me want to gag.

I closed my eyes and tried to ignore the smells.

"I already asked if there was another position or assignment they could give me for the next few months. They said no. There's nothing more I can do," Dad said with a sigh.

"I don't know what to tell her. Don't they understand? It's your daughter," Mom said in a soft voice. A pot clanked and Mom sucked in a breath.

It sounded like they were arguing. About me?

"I know. I can be with you for the next couple of days, but I have to fly out again in two weeks, and between now and then I have to stay late every night." Dad's voice rose louder.

My heart sank down to my shoes. Dad was leaving again? How could he?

"I don't understand," Mom said with a frustrated sigh. A cupboard shut softly and a dish clanked lightly on the counter.

"Vanessa, you know I want to be with her, and with you,

during everything," Dad said, his voice soft and gentle. "But I can't lose this job, now more than ever. We need the insurance."

I didn't want to listen anymore. I couldn't believe it. How could Dad not be there for me?

"*I* know that, but does Jessa?" Mom asked.

"I'll do what I have to do to make it up to her." Dad sighed.

Mom rinsed her pan and took the phone off speaker. As she walked past me into the hallway the smell of garlic and veggies trailed her.

I shut my eyes and held my breath. I didn't want to smell the food. And I didn't want her to know I'd heard her conversation.

Chapter 17

I stayed home from school the week between my first and second chemo treatments. I lived in my bed or on the couch downstairs. I kept trying to get back to Dreamland, but I wasn't able to.

The second treatment was much worse. Dad wasn't able to come with us to the hospital, which made everything harder. Even though I knew he had good reasons, I was still frustrated. His distractions always made me laugh. I threw up several times during the treatment and a few times on the drive home. I stumbled up to my bed when we got home and went straight to sleep.

Something woke me in the middle of the night. The sky was still dark and the moon shone through the blinds in my window. Dad stood in my doorway watching me sleep. He'd still been at work when we'd gotten home.

I sat up and Dad walked in and sat on my bed.

"How are you doing, baby girl?" He scooped me up into his lap.

"Tired," I mumbled into his chest.

"How'd your treatment go?"

"Bad," I whispered. "I missed you."

"I know, honey." He sighed and held me tighter. "I wanted to be there. But I'm swamped at work." He sounded like he was holding back tears.

I remembered the conversation I'd heard him and Mom have. "You're leaving town again?"

He pulled me away from him to look into my eyes. "How'd you know?"

"I heard you and Mom talk about it." I had tried not to think about it. I kept hoping his trip would be canceled. Dad was my rock. He was always there to pick me up when I needed it. "How long is your trip? When do you leave?"

He sighed again. I rested my head on his shoulder. "It's going to be three weeks, and I'm leaving next week. I'll head up with you, but you'll drop me off at the airport before you go to the hospital for chemo."

My chest tightened. "You won't be there for the next CT scan?"

Dad grew very still. "No." His voice cracked on that small word.

He felt awful, I could tell. But he was leaving when I needed him the most. My eyes burned. My silence held my tears in as well. I crawled out of his lap and back under my covers, trying to hide the hurt surging through me. When I could trust my voice I whispered, "Okay."

Dad put his head in his hands and whispered, "I'm sorry, Jessa."

I couldn't respond. He stayed on my bed while I silently cried myself back to sleep.

THE TREE HOUSE swayed in the wind and my heart sank. I wanted to go back to my observatory and look at the stars.

The chalkboard I'd made last time was still hanging on the wall, but a new note was scrawled on it in Sidney's handwriting.

Meet me in the hideout.

~S

After erasing the message, I took the fireman's pole down the tree house and made my way to the waterfall. Thankfully, the cove around the waterfall sheltered me from the wind and I was able to fly into the entrance safely.

Sidney sat at one of the tables in the entrance of the cave. "How are you doing?" she asked.

I plopped down into a beanbag someone had shoved into a corner. "Not great."

"Want to talk about it?" Sidney's eyes held genuine concern in them.

I took a stuttering breath, still trying to hold the tears in from earlier. Not trusting my voice, I shrugged. Sidney joined me on the bean bag and pulled me into a hug, and before I knew it, tears streamed down my face. I pulled away from her and put my face in my hands. Sidney set her hand on my back and the words spilled out of my mouth. I told her about the conversation I'd had with my dad and how sick I felt because of chemo. I even told her how Alexa had been distant since my diagnosis.

When I finished, she put her arm around me. "I'm sorry this is happening to you," she said.

I laid my head on her shoulder and wiped the tears from my cheeks. "Thanks." I inhaled deeply. My heart felt lighter. Again, she hadn't fixed any of my problems, but talking about them had helped.

"Sorry to unload on you," I said, wiping my puffy cheeks and lying back on the bean bag.

"Don't worry about it," Sidney said. "What are friends for, right?"

I nodded thinking of the friends I'd made here. "We need to help the other kids here. Have you had any ideas on how to trick Mr. Black into letting everyone go?"

"I've been thinking about that," Sidney replied. "What if we don't need to trick him? What if we need to help him?"

"What do you mean?" I asked, sitting up on my elbows.

"When Rafa told us about the dragon and the unicorn, he said dark things manifest when you don't find the good thing Dreamland creates for you."

I nodded. "So, we need to find a tiny unicorn for him to choke on."

Sidney laughed. "No, but maybe he just never found his good thing."

"That might be it," I agreed. "Maybe we can figure out what Dreamland made for him and make sure he finds it."

Sidney continued excitedly, "Then he can be happy and Dreamland can heal."

"What new things have shown up in the last couple of months?" I asked.

Sidney closed her eyes and concentrated, "The observatory, a water slide on the north side of the island, the zip line, and I've seen handful of new video games. Do any of those seem like something that Mr. Black would like?"

"Maybe the zip line?" I wondered. "Wait. Didn't Rafa say something about a bridge?"

"That's right," Sidney exclaimed as she stood up, "by the little river in the forest. But why would Dreamland give him a bridge?"

"I have no idea. Grownups are weird sometimes. Do you know any kids who would have wanted it?"

Sidney shook her head. "No. Let's go check it out." She pulled me to my feet.

We exited the cave and began to fly toward the forest, holding each other's hands through the wind. As we approached the river, the bridge was easy to spot from the air. Though small, it was a magnificent structure. Instead of a rope bridge like so many others in Dreamland, this was a solid, stone bridge with expertly crafted arches through which the river passed. The rails were unlike any bridge I had ever seen before; they appeared to be covered in brass and silver scales.

We landed on the ground at one end of the bridge but didn't dare to step out onto it. Like so many other parts of Dreamland, the bridge was already deteriorating and looked unstable. I looked at the rails and saw the brass and silver were not scales at all but thousands and thousands of padlocks. The rails had a wire grid, and the padlocks were locked around almost every available inch of the wires.

"I've seen something like this before," Sidney gasped. "On a travel show."

"Really?" I asked, surprised.

"I've spent a lot of time in bed," she laughed. "Sometimes I'm bored enough to watch travel shows. They're better than soap operas."

"That's true," I agreed.

"This happens a lot in Europe, especially in Paris. Couples put their names on the padlock and throw away the key as a symbol of their love. Paris had to shut the whole practice down because the weight of all the locks was a danger to the bridges."

I gasped. "My mom said Mr. and Mrs. Black had purchased tickets to Paris only a few weeks before she died. And on the first day of school I saw a padlock on Mr. Black's desk with the Eiffel Tower on it. This has to be what Dreamland made for him."

"I've got a good feeling about this," Sidney smiled. "This is going to work."

"If it doesn't, I still vote we find a tiny unicorn."

We laughed in the excitement of our new plan, but then Sidney became serious again.

"We have to get him here," Sidney remarked. "But how?"

I WOKE up to a dark and empty room. A prickling heat washed over my body, and the back of my throat burned. Without warning I threw up all over myself and my bed. Over and over, I retched and cried until Dad came into my room. He turned the light on and rushed over.

He picked me up, not caring about getting puke on himself, and helped me to the bathroom. I crawled in the bathtub and he handed me a bowl to puke in. He murmured "It's okay, baby girl," over and over while rubbing my back. When I'd gone several minutes without throwing up, Dad left and Mom came in and helped me undress and wrap up my PICC line so I could shower. Once I started my shower, she took all my dirty clothes away.

I ran my fingers through my hair as I rinsed it. I could feel the hair sticking to my fingers. I looked down to clean it off and I almost screamed.

Thick clumps of hair hung from my hand.

I ran my hand through my hair again.

More big clumps of hair came away.

My chest tightened.

No, no, no.

I thought I had more time before this happened.

I wanted to hit something.

Water sloshed around my feet. I looked at the bathtub floor.

The drain was clogged with my long, brown hair causing the tub to fill.

The hot water pounded down on my back, heedless of the tears streaming down my cheeks.

Mom cracked the door open. "Jessa? Are you okay?"

I didn't answer. I just stood there, sobbing.

Mom walked over to the shower door. "Were you sick again? Are you done with your shower? I brought you a dryer towel."

I stifled another sob as I mechanically turned off the water. Mom handed the towel through a crack in the door. It was fresh from the dryer—warm and soft. I wrapped myself up in it and opened the door.

Hair clung to my foot as I stepped out of the tub.

Mom looked down and gasped. "Oh, *mijita!*" She pulled me into a hug, soaking her clothes, but she didn't seem to mind. She held me tight for a long moment and let me cry.

"We knew this would happen," she whispered into my hair.

My thinning hair.

"But that doesn't make it any easier," she whispered. She held me tighter until my breathing slowed. "I'm so sorry, *nena.*"

"I didn't know it'd happen this soon." My voice squeaked on the last word.

She hugged me even tighter. "I know this is hard, and it sucks. It really does." She leaned back to look at me. Between the steamy bathroom and my tears, I couldn't see her very well. I tried to blink away the tears, but more kept filling my eyes.

"I'm just so angry," I said, trying to keep my voice steady.

"Come here." Mom walked me to my bedroom and waited with her back turned while I pulled on my robe.

"There's something I want you to hear," she said.

"Okay," I said.

"Really listen, *nena,* this is important."

I nodded, looking right into her mahogany eyes.

She put both hands on my cheeks and looked right back into my watery eyes.

"In Spanish there are two verbs for *to be*. The verb *soy* is a permanent state, like, *I am tall. Estoy* is a temporary state, like *I am sad.*" She wiped the tears from my face and kissed both cheeks. "I want you to know that it's okay to be mad about this.

It's okay to be angry and sad. Because someday, you *will* be happy again. Right now—this"—she pulled my hair over one shoulder—"this sucks. You have every right to be sad and angry. But try to think of those as *estoy* emotions. They're temporary. Don't let them define who you are."

I nodded. Dad had taught me to be strong and brave. He'd helped me build up my shell. But having Mom give me permission to be angry and sad right now—knowing I didn't *have* to be strong every second—helped ease the pain. I was still angry, and that was okay.

Chapter 18

Saturday morning, I woke up to a halo of loose hair on my pillow. The sight of it made me gag. I ran to the bathroom. Every time I closed my eyes, I saw the clumps of hair on my pillow or clogging the drain.

Someone knocked. "Jessa? Are you okay?" Kate asked.

"Go away," I said. I stood in front of the sink, holding on to both sides like my life, or sanity, depended on it. I didn't dare look in the mirror.

Another knock. "Mom wants me to check on you."

"I'm fine." I tried to keep my voice steady but it caught.

"Please let me in," Kate begged.

The fear in her voice caught my attention. I squeezed the sink and took a couple of breaths. I forced myself to look in the mirror. Aside from the dark circles around my eyes, I looked about the same. I wasn't bald yet—despite the quantity of hair I'd found.

I opened the door and Kate came in.

"Did you puke again?" Kate asked, scooting behind me. "Mom wants to know." She sat down on the closed toilet lid; her wide eyes trained on me. She looked older.

"No." I closed my eyes and sighed. My nose and eyes started burning. I didn't want to cry in front of Kate. She was too little to see all of this. I pinched the bridge of my nose. After another long sigh I felt in control enough to face her.

Before I opened my eyes, she'd wrapped herself around me in one of her big hugs. "I'm sorry you're sick." She sniffed.

"Are you crying?" I asked.

She buried her face into me and shook her head.

I untangled myself from her and squatted down to give her a real hug. Her brown eyes were watery and her cheeks were wet. I grabbed a few squares of toilet paper and wiped her face, then I pulled her into a proper hug. "Want to talk about it?"

She shrugged.

I held her close. Her hair smelled like strawberry shampoo. Mom bought her the tear-free kind because Kate still managed to get soap in her eyes. She was so young. I wasn't sure how she compared to other six-year-olds, but compared to me, she was practically a baby.

"Are you going to die?" Her whisper was muffled, and I didn't understand what she'd said for a moment. When the question registered in my mind, I held her tighter.

Something inside me flared up. I was the victim of this disease, but I needed to be strong, now. For Kate.

"No, I'm going to get better. The cancer I have is very beatable, and I have good doctors. Besides, there's no way I'm going to miss out on seeing you get your black belt."

Kate smiled at me, then pulled away. "Are you going to go bald?"

Pulling from the strength I'd just found. I looked her square in the eyes. "No," I said. Her eyes went wide. "I'm not going to let cancer steal my happiness; and I'm not going to let cancer steal my hair either."

"But I thought chemo makes your hair fall out." She reached out and touched my hair.

"It will. But I'm not going to let it fall out. I'm going to shave it off first. Cancer's got nothing on me." I felt strong. I felt in control of something. "Let's go talk to Mom."

Kate and I walked down to the kitchen. Sarah sat at the table watching the latest hair tutorial on her favorite YouTube channel. Mom was reading a parenting book while Dad made breakfast for everyone—he made the *best* eggs.

"Any chance we can get a few slices of bacon with those eggs, Dad?" Sarah asked, with hope in her voice.

"Sorry Sarah-bean," Dad said with a smile. "All the health books say it's important to keep a healthy diet to give our immune systems the best possible chance."

"Oh, okay," Sarah replied. "That's cool."

Dad had been reading health books with any extra time he had. He hadn't gone climbing or done any of his usual hobbies for weeks. Mom spent her spare moments with her nose in a book or on the Internet, learning everything she could about Hodgkin's and how to be the best caregiver possible. Even Sarah and Kate were being impacted as each health decision Mom and Dad made was applied to the whole family and not just me. Nobody complained, though.

In that moment, it struck me how much my family was working together to fight this in whatever way they could. This wasn't only my fight. Sure, I was the patient, but I had an entire support team helping me. I couldn't fight just for Kate or even myself. I needed to fight for my whole family.

The smells of breakfast nauseated me, but I pushed through the feeling and walked up to Mom. Kate held my hand as we waited for Mom to bookmark her spot.

"How are you feeling, *mijita*?" She looked tired and worn.

"Jessa's going to shave her head!" Kate blurted out.

Mom cocked an eyebrow at me but turned her focus to Kate. "Really?"

"Yep." Kate smiled. "She said she's not going to let cancer steal her hair."

Mom turned toward me. "Is this true?"

My determination wavered, but one look at Kate's smiling face kept me strong. "Yes. I want to shave my head before my hair falls out."

A loud clank followed by a sharp intake of breath came from the kitchen. We all turned to look at Dad. He dashed to the sink and shoved his hand under the running water. "Burned my hand."

Mom moved to check it out.

Sarah came into the room and sat on the couch where Mom vacated. "I heard what you said," she told me. "I think it's really cool. I have a couple of cute headbands you can have, if you want."

"Really?" I asked.

Sarah nodded.

"Thanks" was all I could manage to get out.

"I know other people shave their heads to support people with cancer—but I'm not going to," Sarah said. "I don't think I'd look good bald. But I'll cut it short and donate the hair to help other cancer patients."

"You can't cut your hair," I said in shock.

"I will for you. You're going to kick cancer's butt, and I want you to know I'm with you, every step of the way—even if I don't go bald for you." She smiled at me. "Besides, I've always wanted to try a pixie cut."

"Me too!" Kate chimed in.

Mom came over. "Sounds like we're heading to the salon today." Her eyes brimmed with tears.

I couldn't find the right words to say. I wiped my face with a tissue and pulled Kate and Sarah into a tight hug. I'd never realized how incredible my sisters were.

THE STYLIST PULLED my hair into a ponytail, then braided it. Another stylist on the left did the same for Sarah while Kate sat in the chair to my right. I still couldn't believe Sarah was cutting her hair. I couldn't remember the last time she'd cut it.

The sound of clipping made me focus on the mirror in front of me.

Snip, snip, snip.

The stylist pulled the braid away as wisps of hair fell around my face. She set the braid down and started trimming my hair down—she'd explained how she couldn't start by buzzing it; there were a few steps before that.

I looked different with short hair. I hadn't worn it short since preschool, and never this short. I was being transformed. Part of me wanted to play with it while it was short. But quicker than I expected, the stylist pulled out her clippers. Mom stood behind me, watching. She'd taken a few pictures of us. I held her gaze through the mirror as the buzzing came near my head.

Bzzz, bzzz, bzzz.

It took a few passes. I couldn't watch the mirror. I focused on Mom, reminding myself that this was my choice. Mom's eyes held mine. I could tell she wanted to watch the stylist, but she kept eye contact with me. And I felt like she held me up.

"Okay, you're done." The stylist stepped away.

I reached up and touched it. My head felt fuzzy. I shivered. The room was colder. Everyone stared at me.

"I guess we'll save money on shampoo," I said to break the tension.

Everyone laughed.

Chapter
19

M y doctors said I needed to limit going out in public as much as possible so I wouldn't get an infection. The whole family needed to be very careful. Everyone washed their hands and changed their clothes when they got home from work or school. Mom was taking no chances. She even signed me up for online school.

My life consisted of home, the car, and the hospital. Dreamland was the only place I could escape, and things weren't great there anymore. I'd improved my appearance-changing skills, though I still struggled.

Alexa didn't have much contact with me, but after several texts begging her to break up the boredom, she finally agreed to come.

When the doorbell rang, I was lying on the couch working my way through the next season of my latest Netflix binge.

"I'll get it," Sarah offered.

But I was already up off the couch. "I got it. It's Alexa."

Sarah nodded and headed up to her room.

Though I was sick and very tired, I wanted to jump up and down with excitement. I hadn't seen Alexa for what felt like months. It'd be like old times. Just me and Alexa.

I opened the door and my heart sank to my knees. Carleigh and Alexa stood on my doorstep. Carleigh looked, as always, like she'd stepped off the runway of a teen fashion show. And Alexa looked as though she'd shopped out of Carleigh's closet. I felt frumpy in my old sweatpants and oversized hoodie.

"How are you?" Alexa asked.

"I'm doing okay. Come in." I stepped back to let them in.

They both walked in and stood awkwardly in the entryway until I led them into the family room.

Carleigh seemed like she held her breath. Did it smell bad? Was it me? Alexa plopped onto the couch and I sat down next to her. Carleigh parked herself on the arm of the recliner as though she didn't want to touch anything.

I pulled on a mask. "Sorry, I don't want to catch any germs. Do you mind sanitizing?" I handed Alexa a bottle of hand sanitizer, which she promptly used and handed off to Carleigh.

"We miss you at school," Alexa said, and my heart warmed. "How's online school?"

"It's not bad. I can stay in my pajamas all day."

"Clearly." Carleigh raised her eyebrows and gave my ratty old sweats a once-over.

My cheeks burned. "I'll be right back." If I changed into regular clothes, maybe I wouldn't feel so uncomfortable around them. I stood up and walked to my room. I had the perfect outfit. Mom had sprung for a brand-new shirt, and Sarah had used her own money to buy me a stylish pair of jeans.

I changed as fast as I could and then started down the stairs. I slowed when I heard Alexa and Carleigh speaking.

"Can we go yet?" Carleigh asked. "I'm supposed to meet up with Drew."

"My mom said we have to stay for at least twenty minutes," Alexa said. "You know how she gets."

My insides froze.

"Maybe we can leave early and your mom can meet us on the corner," Carleigh said. "Jessa creeps me out. I can't believe she's bald and not covering it up with a wig."

"Did you notice she doesn't have eyebrows or eyelashes?" Alexa asked.

"Yeah, it's disgusting. She looks so weird."

I couldn't move.

I couldn't breathe.

Their words started to jumble in my ears. I took the stairs back to my room and shut the door. What could I do? How could I face them after what I'd heard? Tears started flowing as I buried my head in my pillow.

The kids' phone buzzed from the pocket of the sweatpants I'd just changed out of. I picked them up off the floor and dug the phone out. I wasn't supposed to take it in my room, but I'd forgotten it was there.

I wiped my eyes and checked the screen. It wasn't from one of my contacts—just a random number. I opened the message. A gif of a dancing piece of chocolate filled the screen. At the bottom of the image the words **Have a speCHOCular day!** danced along with the chocolate. As I held the phone and watched the image dance, another message came in. **I ran into your mom at the grocery store and asked for a number to text you at. This is Michael, by the way.**

The next message popped up. **I hope the dancing chocolate can brighten your day.**

I sniffed and thought about what Michael had said about Carleigh. He was right. She wasn't a good friend. I wasn't ready to talk to either of them right now, though.

Sarah was the only other person at home. I pulled up a message to her and typed in the family code.

X

Sarah responded right away. **What do you need?**

Can you ask Alexa and Carleigh to leave? I'm not feeling well. I didn't want to tell her what I'd heard.

No problem.

The floor creaked with each step Sarah took as she walked down the hall. She paused on the stairs for a moment before continuing to the bottom.

"You think you can talk about my sister like that?" Sarah's voice cut through the air.

Alexa mumbled something I couldn't hear.

"How dare you!" Sarah yelled. "Get! Out!"

I heard scrambling and a few hasty words.

"You're supposed to be her best friend." Sarah's voice dropped a little but remained loud enough that I could still hear every word.

The door slammed, and my tears returned. I crawled under my blankets. I couldn't stop my mind from replaying what they said about me.

The doorbell rang, and I heard muffled voices. Had Alexa come back? Had her mom brought her?

My door opened and I heard footsteps.

"I don't want to talk about it," I said, hoping I was talking to Sarah and not Alexa and her mom.

"Your friends are jerks." Sarah's voice had a soft tone to it, one I rarely heard from her.

I sat up and took a shuddering breath but continued facing the wall.

Before I knew it, Sarah was hugging me from behind. "I love you, Jessa." Sarah let go of me and climbed onto the bed. She picked up my stuffed unicorn and held it on her lap. "But if I ever see those girls again—" she started.

"Don't," I interrupted. "Please don't do anything. And don't tell Mom."

"Why are you defending them?" Sarah gripped the unicorn so tight her knuckles turned white.

"They're my friends," I said. "At least, Alexa is."

"Those girls are not your friends. Maybe Alexa used to be, but real friends don't treat each other that way." She had a fire in her eyes and a bite to her words. "Those girls are selfish and mean. You deserve better. Do you understand?"

I lay back down on my bed, feeling drained and too tired to argue. "Okay."

"Now that we have that out of the way..." Sarah stood and walked to my nightstand. She picked up a bulky envelope and handed it to me. "Sidney's dad dropped this off for you."

When Sarah left the room, I tore it open. Inside was Sidney's beaded bracelet and a note.

Jessa,

Sorry it took so long to get this to you. Mom and Dad have stayed with me at the hospital, but Dad needed to go home so I'm sending it with him now.

I wanted to give you my bracelet. I feel like it always gives me strength when I need it. These are some of my favorite beads and I wanted to share them with you. Thanks for being my friend. I'm sorry you've got cancer. It really sucks, and it's not fair. I hope you get better soon. Come visit me next time you're at Children's. I'm in room 204.

Xoxo
Sidney

I fingered the biggest yellow bead in the middle—the one with the 'S' on it. My heart felt big. Sidney was a great friend. She had worked hard for each of these beads. My vision got blurry. I tried to blink the tears away, but they stayed.

Then I remembered how when I'd first heard about her diagnosis it scared me. I stopped being friends with her because I didn't know how to act around someone with cancer. Had I treated Sidney the same way Alexa was treating me now? My big heart deflated. Why hadn't I ever gone to visit her? She'd had cancer, almost continuously, since kindergarten. She must have felt so lonely.

I put the bracelet on my wrist and lay on my bed. I wanted to cry for myself because I had cancer. Because of what Carleigh and Alexa said. Because Sarah defended me. For Sidney and her kindness, and the years of friendship I'd missed out on with her. But I'd already cried all of my tears. My eyes felt swollen and sore. I tried to sniff, but I couldn't breathe through my clogged nose. I flipped my pillow over. The cool fabric soothed my hot face.

The rhythmic sound of the fan calmed me.

I closed my eyes.

THE BREEZE WAS COOL. The sky outside the tree house window was dark but calm. I flew out into the open air. Would Sidney be here tonight? I wanted to find her and tell her how sorry I was. To thank her for not giving up on me and forgiving me.

Despite what happened with Alexa and Carleigh and how sad I felt when I fell asleep, flying was simple. I could almost feel a connection to Sidney emanating from the bracelet, lifting me up and bringing me hope.

In the distance, the large black pirate ship floated in the area where we'd seen Mr. Black's bridge. I flew low to the ground, hoping to avoid being seen by Mr. Black. Dark clouds surrounded the mountain, and mist swirled over the river.

I made good time to the bridge. But when I arrived, I hesitated to approach it. I landed in a tree right outside of the fog to rest. My gut twisted with more than just nerves.

Something felt wrong. I couldn't put my finger on it, but I could feel it in my bones.

Thunder rumbled in the distance.

Something red flashed across the river.

Mr. Black was here.

I jumped from the tree and flew across the river, landing in a tree on the other side. Heavy boots stomped through the woods, crashing through twigs and bushes. Was he coming to the bridge? Lightning flashed in the distance. A drop of rain landed on my head.

"Mr. Black, over here!" I heard Sidney shout. I was relieved to hear her voice. She was close by but still obscured by the mist. I floated down to the ground, landing near the tree.

The bridge creaked. Sidney stood just inside of it, facing me with Mr. Black between us, looking at Sidney. I took a step toward them, but Sidney met my eyes and gave a slight shake of her head.

"What are you doing out in this weather?" Mr. Black's voice sounded concerned. "You're sick."

"Do you recognize this bridge?" Sidney asked. She stepped farther onto the bridge, which groaned loudly.

More raindrops fell around me. My heart raced. Was it safe for her to stand on the bridge? It looked even more unstable than last time.

"I don't think so." Mr. Black stepped closer to Sidney. "You need to come to the sick room, though." Worry filled his voice as he spoke.

Mr. Black stepped onto the bridge, but their combined weight was too much. A crack as loud as thunder filled the air. The locks from the bridge fell into the water with a splash. Sidney stumbled forward and Mr. Black grabbed her arm and pulled her to the shore just as the bridge collapsed beneath her.

Before I could react, the ghostly pirate ship floated toward them. A ramp was lowered, and Mr. Black started ushering Sidney toward the ramp.

"Wait," Sidney said, trying to pull her arm from his grasp. "I'm not sick. I'm okay."

Mr. Black didn't stop. "If you're feeling better, then you can go to class with the rest of the kids."

Sidney pulled but couldn't get out of his grip.

"Stop!" he yelled. A crash of lightning struck behind us.

Sidney stopped struggling. The color drained from her face, and her chin trembled.

I flew toward the ship. I couldn't let Mr. Black take her.

"That's better," he said. "I know you're sick. You need the sick room."

Sidney turned to look at me as I approached them from behind. Fear gleamed in her eyes.

A door slammed downstairs.

No, no, no. I couldn't wake up now.

I focused on things around me. The cool air.

The breeze of my ceiling fan.

No. The drops of rain pelting my body.

The soft pillow underneath my head. I could feel my body shifting. My stomach hurt. I needed to use the bathroom.

I landed and tried to focus on the sensations I felt in Dreamland. I touched the bracelet, hoping it would help.

Mr. Black held Sidney's wrist as he pulled the ramp into the ship. Horror pulsed through me as the ship floated up into the air and the wind picked up. They sailed away as I faded out.

My eyes popped open, and my heart ached.

The pain from the waking world overwhelmed me. My bowels hurt; I felt nauseated. My skin felt feverish.

I ran to the bathroom, trying desperately to hold everything in until I got to the toilet.

Chapter
20

The next morning was Halloween. I had always gone trick-or-treating with Alexa and Kate. Today I didn't want to talk to anyone. I couldn't stop thinking about Sidney. I tried texting her mom, but she didn't answer.

After school, Sarah invited me to watch a movie with her while Mom took Kate trick-or-treating. I made sure I stayed out of sight of the front door while Sarah handed out candy.

Dad spent the evening packing for his long trip. We would take him to the airport in the morning, then head to the hospital for another CT scan. If my bloodwork looked good, I'd have another round of chemo.

At some point during the night, Michael came to the door, and Sarah let him in.

He handed me a bag full of candy. "That's half of my candy. I figured you wouldn't be able to go this year, so I brought you some." He was dressed in a suit with a bow tie. Taped to his chest was a paper with the word *Sorry* written in big block letters.

I took the candy he handed to me. "Thanks." My voice cracked and I swallowed a lump in my throat. Sarah stood behind him, with a half-smile on her lips. I cleared my throat. "What in the world are you dressed up as?" I asked, grateful that my voice came out normal.

"What am I wearing?" Michael spun slowly in a circle, with his arms out.

"A suit?" I guessed.

"Formal wear," Sarah said.

Michael pointed at her. "Bingo." He turned back toward me. "Now what does the paper say?"

"Sorry. So, it's an apology?" I guessed.

"Now put them together." He raised his eyebrows expectantly.

And then it hit me. "You're a formal apology?" I guessed.

Sarah snorted.

"That's right," Michael said. His big smile warmed my heart.

I laughed too. It felt so much better to laugh than to worry.

"Anyway, I gotta go. My dad and little brother are waiting for me." He picked up his candy bag and backed away. "I hope I can see you at school soon."

"Thanks for the candy," I called. He looked over his shoulder and waved as he walked out.

"He seems nice." Sarah cocked an eyebrow at me and my cheeks flushed.

"He is," I said, ignoring the smile on her face. I turned back to the movie but didn't really pay attention to the rest of it. The stark difference between Alexa's and Carleigh's visit and Michael's visit wasn't lost on me. I hadn't changed since yesterday. I was still bald and in my pajamas, but I hadn't once been uncomfortable around Michael. Having cancer was something I never would have picked for myself, but somehow it had brought me some amazing new friends.

The next morning, we left at six a.m. so Dad could catch his flight. I tried to sleep for most of the drive up, but I couldn't get comfortable.

Dad drove us to the airport. He kissed me on the head, gave Mom a long hug, and told us he'd message us when he landed.

Mom hopped in the driver's seat, and the two of us drove to the hospital.

We checked in and they gave me a big bottle of contrast to drink.

I threw up after the first two cups. Mom handed me a cup of water to rinse my mouth. My throat burned.

"I don't know if I can do this," I said. "I miss Dad. He's supposed to be here with me." I still couldn't believe he had left on his trip.

Mom gave me a hug. "I'm sorry, *mijita*. You're strong, you're brave, you can do hard things. Remember?"

I nodded but it wasn't the same coming from Mom. My hands shook as I took another cup of contrast from Mom.

This time I used a straw and plugged my nose while I drank. It worked. I still tasted it, but it was less foul than before.

"How about we try one cup every five minutes?" Mom suggested. "Then you can relax a bit in between."

"Okay," I agreed. As I sat in the waiting room with my stomach churning, I couldn't help thinking of Sidney. Was she okay in Dreamland? "Can you ask Mrs. Thatcher if we can visit today?" I asked.

"That's a great idea. I'm sure Sidney would love to see you," Mom said. "I'll text Hannah right now."

I choked another cup of contrast down, and it almost came back up.

Mom's phone rang and she answered. "Hey, how's it going?"

I couldn't help but touch the bracelet. Sidney was at the hospital somewhere.

"Here she is," Mom said, handing me the phone. "It's Dad."

"Hi," I said.

"How's the contrast going?" His voice came across soft and difficult to hear because of the background noise from the airport.

"Gross. I already threw up twice." I shifted in my chair to hold the phone better. "How's the airport?"

"Security was fast today. Now I've got to wait two hours until boarding." He cleared his throat. "I've got one for you: if an elephant doesn't matter would it be an irrelephant?"

I laughed. "You earned that one."

He didn't speak for a moment and his voice grew serious when he started talking. "I'm sorry I'm not there with you." He sighed. "The truth is, if I don't work extra hard, I might lose this job. And I need this job to make sure we can pay for your treatments."

I nodded. "I know, Dad. It's okay," I said automatically. And I realized, it *was* okay. Dad wasn't abandoning me. He was taking care of me. It just looked different than what I'd imagined. "It really is okay. I know you want to be here. Sorry I wasn't very nice about it before."

"Thanks, sweetie." His voice sounded shaky. "That means a lot," he whispered.

"Want to talk to Mom?" I asked.

"Sure. I love you, Jessa." Dad took a slow breath. "You're a good girl."

"Love you, Daddy." I handed the phone to Mom. She swapped me for another cup of contrast.

I plugged my nose and sipped it until I could see the bottom of the cup. I could do this.

THE SCANS WENT WELL, and the doctors okayed me for chemo. I wasn't feeling great, but Mom and I decided we'd rather get it done now than later.

We checked into oncology, and they pulled me back into the chemo room, where they accessed my PICC line and pushed a bunch of fluids into it. They gave me an iPad to play on while I waited. None of the games interested me. I couldn't stop thinking of Sidney.

Mom's phone dinged, indicating she'd gotten a text. She furrowed her eyebrows as she read it.

"Is it from Mrs. Thatcher?"

Mom nodded, typing in a response.

"What did she say?" I asked.

"She says we can go visit Sidney."

I wanted to jump up into the air but I settled for a thumbs up.

I shivered. The pre-chemo fluids always chilled me. Mom stepped out and came back with warm blankets.

The nurse came in after a while and started injecting all the different medicines into my PICC line. About half way through I started feeling nauseous. I groaned and Mom was right there with the puke bag.

"Let me give you something to help," the nurse said as she drew up another syringe and shot it into my IV.

I lay down and closed my eyes, but the nausea didn't go away. Mom sat down next to me and rubbed my back.

After only a few moments I felt the world swaying around me. I opened my eyes. I lay in one of the hammocks in the tree house. The movement around me made me feel dizzy. Was the hammock swinging? I climbed out of it, but I continued to rock back and forth. The wind was still; why was the tree house still moving?

I looked around at the state of it. The boards that made up the walls and floor were rotten and broken. All of the visible tree limbs had large, black gashes on them. Memories of the rotting arboretum and Mr. Black's bridge breaking flashed through my mind bringing me to one conclusion: I needed to get out of the tree house before it collapsed.

A loud creak sounded below me, and the tree house shuddered.

The noise was almost drowned out by the thudding of my heart in my ears. I floated off the floor and made my way slowly to the door. Any movement might trigger it.

Another loud groan from below, and I flew into the open air.

The black clouds blocked any hope of light except the occasional flash of lightning.

A deafening crack followed by the sound of splintering wood filled my ears.

I flew straight up into the sky as the tree crashed to the ground, taking down a few of the neighboring trees. My heart beat so hard, it felt as though it might leap from my chest.

Lightning struck nearby, momentarily blinding me. I dropped back down below the tops of the trees. I couldn't fly until the lightning storm had passed.

The ground was covered in tree limbs and broken planks. Fear ran through my veins and squeezed my heart. I stood in the rubble, unable to move.

What would we do without the tree house? Where would I appear in Dreamland?

Why did I think I could fix this? I wasn't brave.

My dad's voice broke through my thoughts. *Courage comes when you're scared and you face your fears anyway.*

He was right when I had my first CT scan, and he'd tell me the same thing now.

I forced myself to put one foot in front of the other and the words ran through my head with each step. *I am brave, I am strong, I can do hard things.*

My heart slowed as I moved away from the fallen tree house. And soon enough I didn't have to pretend to be brave or strong. Lightning still flashed through the sky, so I continued on foot.

The air on my bald head made me shiver. I hadn't realized that I didn't have hair here. I stopped walking and thought about what my hair had looked like, forcing myself to really focus on it. My scalp prickled making goosebumps pop up all over me. Keeping the picture of my hair in my mind, I reached up and touched my head. Hair had sprouted from my bald head and was growing longer and longer. I felt it tickle my neck and watched as bangs covered my eyes. It stopped growing after a minute and I let my hands flow through it. With a lighter heart, I continued on. I was getting better at changing my appearance.

The lightning storm had moved to the other side of the island by the time I reached the beach. The wind was still. I needed to help Sidney.

Thunder boomed behind me in the distance as I flew into the open air above the ocean. I felt a pull toward Skull Island. Was Mr. Black still there? The thought made me want to turn around and head to the hideout.

But he had Sidney. I needed to help her and all the other kids. I took a breath to calm the butterflies inside me. It didn't do much, though.

I flew low to the ground and followed the pull toward Skull Island. The waves below were like hands reaching up to get me. They smashed into each other, splashing me with icy water. When I looked down, I saw a mermaid, but she looked much different from the one who'd rescued me last time.

Her hair was made up of writhing eels that sparked with electricity when they bumped into each other. Her pale skin shimmered in the water. She gave me a hungry smile, showing sharp pointed teeth. I recoiled.

Too late, I realized I was flying lower than I should. A wave crashed over me, and I fell into the water.

The mermaid grabbed me. Instead of warm, helping hands,

her iron grip felt cold and slimy as she pulled me down into the sea.

With all my strength, I tried to pull my arm from her. She held me tighter, all the while dragging me deeper into the murky water.

My breath was running out. It didn't matter how hard I fought; the mermaid was too strong.

Deeper and deeper we went.

My ears felt like they'd burst from the pressure around me. Maybe if I died here, I would just wake up.

The thought of Sidney trapped by Mr. Black burned inside me. Sidney, who had never hurt me, or anyone. Sidney, who was there for me as much as she could be. She had always known exactly what I'd needed. *She* was a real friend. She had shown me how to be a better friend. I had to be there for her now.

My heart felt like it expanded and warmth flooded through me.

The mermaid screeched as though burned. She jerked her slimy fingers back and released me. I focused on a little patch of light above me and swam as hard as I could. The urge to breathe was stronger than ever. I wasn't going to make it to the surface before I needed air. My lungs burned with every second.

I concentrated hard and thought of being in a giant bubble with breathable air.

To my surprise, it happened. I gasped and coughed. The bubble continued to move toward the surface, but now I could breathe and see. The water around me changed from murky to clear as I moved through it—almost like the bubble was cleansing the water. As I shot out of the water and into the air, my protective bubble popped.

The wind blew harder than ever, but it pushed me toward the island. I flew straight to Skull Island and landed in one of the eye sockets.

I sneaked down the first hall and peeked around the corner. No sign of Mr. Black.

He had said he would take her to the sick room. I hurried past his classroom, wiping my sweaty palms on my jeans as I continued down the hall.

As I approached the office, a jolt of cold shot through my body, and I shivered. I could hear Mom murmur something so quietly that I couldn't understand. The nurse responded.

I couldn't wake up now. As I focused on the school's old gray carpet and the painted brick walls, touching Sidney's bracelet helped me stay grounded.

I started down the hall, stepping as lightly as I could. The sick room was down the hall from the front office and across from the teacher's lounge.

The carpet muffled my footsteps but couldn't quiet my pounding heart.

I passed the windowed office and arrived at the sick room before I knew it. I tried opening the windowless wooden door, but it wouldn't budge. I imagined the lock disappearing. The door still didn't budge. I needed to at least see inside to know if she was there. I closed my eyes, concentrating on making a window in the door. When I opened them, I was surprised to find I had done more than create a window. The sick room door had changed entirely to glass.

Sidney lay peacefully on a bed. She was so still. Her usual headband was askew, making her hair stick up even more.

My insides froze.

Was she asleep?

Behind me, a door shut. I jumped and spun around. Mr. Black had come out of the teacher's lounge.

"What are you doing here?" he asked.

I had been so focused on staying in Dreamland and helping Sidney, I hadn't looked for him.

"I...I..." The words wouldn't come out.

Mr. Black smiled. His eyes were kind, though they seemed hollower than I remembered. "It's nice to see a friendly face. Come and sit down." He opened the door to the teachers' lounge.

Mom shook me. "Jessa, you're done. It's time to get up."

Chapter 21

I opened my eyes in the hospital room. Mom stood with her coat draped on her arm. "Ready to go? Want to pick out another bead?" She held the plastic container out to me.

I grabbed the first one I could. "Mom, can we go see Sidney, now?" My heart raced a mile a minute. I climbed off the table wanting to run to Sidney, but a wave of nausea stopped me in my tracks. Mom stepped closer and steadied me.

"Are you okay?" Mom grabbed a puke bag. "Do you need to sit down?"

"No." I tried to sound firm but it came out more like a croak. "Let's go." I clutched the puke bag and pushed the nausea away as best as I could.

As Mom and I walked to the elevator, I kept picturing Sidney asleep...in Dreamland. What did it mean for her in real life? Could she wake up here? Was she stuck there?

The elevator took forever. Finally, it stopped on her floor and we headed toward her room, 204.

An alarm was sounding, and nurses and doctors were rushing down the hall and into a room. A worker bumped into us. He muttered a hasty apology and jogged into the same room.

A wave of dizziness flooded over me. I couldn't see the number of the room, but I was sure it was Sidney's. A pit formed deep inside me.

Mr. Thatcher hustled past us and stopped dead in his tracks outside Sidney's room.

Mom took my hand and we hurried over to him. "Is she okay?" Mom asked. "Hannah sent me a text a few minutes ago saying we could come by and visit."

"I—I—I don't know. I just left to use the bathroom," he stammered. His face turned from peach to gray in an instant, and he staggered.

Mom put her arm around him and helped him into a chair in the hall facing Sidney's open door.

More workers rushed in and out of her room. Doctors and nurses were calling for medicine and supplies. Mrs. Thatcher stood against the wall inside the room, her face pale and drawn, as a half dozen people rushed around the bed. I could only see Sidney's feet.

I didn't want to watch this anymore but I felt rooted to the spot. I wanted to cover my eyes or turn and run far away. This wasn't happening.

But that was Sidney.

Memories flashed through my mind. Sidney with her short spiky hair, laughing and flying in Dreamland. Of racing games and ice cream fruit—laughing as it melted down our chins. Sidney asleep. Sidney sick.

I wanted to help her. She was asleep in Dreamland. Maybe if she woke up in Dreamland, she'd wake up here, too.

"Mom, can I lie down?" I blurted.

Mom glanced at Mr. Thatcher and murmured, "I'll be right back." She walked down the hall and found a nurse who wasn't rushing toward Sidney's room. They shared a few words, then the nurse came up to me.

"You doin' okay, hun?" She put her hand on my shoulder. "We have an empty bed right over here." She indicated the room next to Sidney's, then glanced at my mom. "Is that okay?"

Mom nodded but glanced back at Mr. Thatcher.

"Go sit with him, Mom. I'll be fine. He could use your help." I went into the room, shut the door, and lay on the bed.

My heart raced. I couldn't stop thinking of her. Was she dying in the room next to me? Was she still trapped and asleep in Dreamland? A million other questions ran through my mind as my heart pounded in my chest.

I'd never had a harder time calming down, but I *needed* to sleep. I took a few deep breaths. I could feel my heart slowing down. After a few more, my hands still shook but I felt a lot calmer. I touched Sidney's bracelet and closed my eyes.

With the tree house ruined, where would I wake up in Dreamland now?

The observatory popped into my mind. I pictured the large telescope dominating the room.

I could feel the pillow under my head—flat with a rough pillow case.

Could I hear the leaves rustling from the trees below?

The scratchy blanket had pilled from being washed thousands of times.

The dome creaked as it opened, and I could almost feel the breeze of the cool night air.

I dared to open my eyes. A sigh of relief escaped my lips when I saw the star chart surrounding me.

I'd made it.

I WALKED THROUGH THE CLEARING, remembering the zipline I'd seen. I needed the fastest route to Sidney I could find, and this was it. I strapped myself into the harness and held my breath. The trees zoomed past me, and I stifled a scream as I plummeted toward the beach. The ride was over quickly, and I stumbled gratefully onto the sand.

Once I'd recovered, I flew across the sea. The bracelet did give me strength, just like Sidney had said. With it, I felt like she flew next to me. I knew I could rescue her. With Sidney, I felt stronger than everything here.

I made good time to Skull Island. When I landed, I ran through the halls, not bothering to duck or be quiet. The door to Mr. Black's room was open, and Rafa waved me down.

"What's going on?" he asked.

I slowed down to catch my breath and walked up to the doorway. "Sidney is in trouble. She and I are friends in real life. She's really sick. I think she might..." I couldn't finish. A lump rose in my throat. I swallowed hard.

Rafa's eyes were wide.

Tears were building behind my eyes. "When I came here a few minutes ago, she was asleep." My voice wavered. "Now she's in trouble in the real world." I finished. "Can you come with me?"

"We're still stuck in here. There's a barrier or something." He tried to stick his hand out of the doorway but it was blocked by something invisible. "Go wake her up," he urged. "She needs you."

I nodded and ran to the office and down the hall. The glass door hadn't changed back to wood. I could see Sidney's light brown hair sticking out from beneath the covers. I checked the teachers' lounge. Mr. Black wasn't in there. I walked up to the sick room door. I wiggled the handle, but it was still locked.

Maybe I could break the glass.

I pictured the glass gone or shattered, but I couldn't concentrate properly. I kept thinking back to Sidney in the hospital.

I knocked on the glass, hoping to get her attention, but she didn't move. I'd have to break the glass manually. I ran to the teachers' lounge and opened the door.

I scanned the room, looking for something, anything, to help break the glass. The stools tucked under the table had metal legs on them. I ran over and picked one up, then sprinted back to Sidney's door. Without thinking about what I was about to do, I swung the stool as hard as I could at the glass door.

With a loud crash, the glass shattered into a million pieces. It rained down on me, cutting me as it fell. I could feel glass slivers in my arms and hands, but I didn't care. I ran through the wreckage to Sidney's side.

"Wake up, Sidney!" I shook her but she didn't stir. "Sidney!"

She didn't respond.

"No, no, no," I muttered. I pulled the covers off of her and threw them on the floor. I shook her shoulders and shouted her name.

But she stayed still.

"Please wake up," I cried. My eyes burned. I knelt down on the covers next to her bed. "Dreamland needs you, and so do I." Tears started to flow in earnest. I dropped my head down, letting my forehead rest on her arm. "Sidney, you are the best part of Dreamland. I'd rather have you than anything else here."

She stirred. I looked up at her, and she opened her eyes. "Jessa?"

"Sidney?" I breathed a sigh of relief. "Are you okay?"

"I was in the most beautiful place." She had a dreamy look in her eyes. "It was even better than Dreamland." She looked around. "Where am I? I thought I was at the hospital."

"We're in Dreamland," I said shakily, relief flooding through me. She was awake. "You were captured."

"Oh, right." She had a half smile on her face, as though being captured was of little importance.

"We have to get out of here before Mr. Black comes back."

"Mr. Black," Sidney said, sitting up. "The bridge broke."

"I know," I said. "I think it was too far gone to help him."

"I think there's some sort of spell on this place so if you get captured here, you always come back here when you wake up." Her eyes widened. "Jessa," she whispered. She stared over my shoulder.

I spun around.

Mr. Black stood in the doorway looking concerned.

"What should we do?" I muttered to Sidney.

"Make a run for it," Sidney answered.

Mr. Black took a step toward us.

"Run! Go!" Sidney shouted.

I bolted across the room and ducked around him. I raced through the halls and past Mr. Black's classroom. When I got to the hall with the lockers, I turned to grab Sidney's hand, but she wasn't there. Where was she? I thought we had run together. But Sidney had stayed behind. I turned to go back, but I felt myself fading.

Mom shook me awake. "Jessa?"

I opened my eyes and sat bolt upright. "Is she okay?"

Through the open door I saw several nurses and doctors filing down the hall past my room.

Mom wiped her wet eyes.

"What happened? What's wrong with Sidney?"

"Her heart stopped. They were able to revive her." Mom glanced toward the hallway.

"But she's okay." I breathed a sigh of relief. "She's going to be okay."

Mom pursed her lips and closed her eyes tight. She looked away from me and sniffed.

"Mom, Sidney is going to be okay, right?"

Mom turned back toward me and took a slow breath before she spoke. "Her kidney and liver functions are too low."

"I don't understand." What did that even mean?

She put her arm around me. "She's okay for now, *nena*, but she isn't going to be here much longer."

"And then? She's going home, right?" Deep down, I knew the answer, but I couldn't believe it.

"Sweetie, Sidney's organs are failing. They're not working the way they're supposed to." Mom pulled me into a tight hug.

"No!" I shouted and pushed Mom away. "You're wrong. She's fine. Her mom said the treatments were working and she was getting better." I couldn't believe this. I wouldn't believe it. What a mean joke for Mom to play on me.

Mom closed her eyes, exhaled a long breath, then opened her eyes. She spoke with a clear and measured tone. "When someone is really sick, they can get better for a little while before they get worse. They think this was one of those times. They did a scan earlier. Sidney's cancer has metastasized."

"What?" I asked.

"It has spread," Mom clarified. "Instead of just in her bones, it's spread to her liver, her lungs, her kidneys...all over her body."

I didn't know what to say. I'd just seen Sidney, and she looked fine. A little woozy but fine.

But that was in Dreamland. How did she look here?

"Can I see her?"

"She's not awake right now. The doctors say she'll sleep a lot over the next week or two before..."

"Before what?" I asked.

Mom held my gaze. "Sidney is dying." She said each word with clarity and love. And each word stabbed my heart.

"She only has a week?" I wanted to hide. I wanted to run. I wanted to fly far away, to cotton candy cloud mazes and butterfly-filled meadows.

"I'm so sorry, *mijita*." Mom pulled me into her, and we cried together.

"Do you want to go see her?" Mom asked.

We had been sitting in the room next to Sidney's for over an hour now. I was starting to feel sick from chemo with the usual stomach cramps, chills, and nausea. And I was afraid to see Sidney—afraid that this would be the last time I saw her alive.

"I don't know," I hedged. The thought of seeing Sidney so sick made my stomach flutter.

"I think you should." Mom kissed my bald head. "I think you'll regret it if you don't."

I nodded. Mom was right, but that didn't make it any less daunting. "Will you come with me?"

"Of course."

We stood up and Mom took my hand. She led me out of my room and into the hall. The smell of the hospital hit me hard in the hallway. I paused and took slow breaths to calm myself. Mom offered to get me a soda to settle my stomach, but I declined. I wasn't sure I could keep anything down right now.

We walked into Sidney's room. I wanted to run to her. I wanted to run away. Fear flooded through me, into my limbs and chest until I thought I'd burst with it or crumple to the ground.

Sidney lay on the bed hooked up to so many different machines. Several had blinking lights or emitted beeps now and then. Her oxygen tank made a rhythmic breathing noise. I followed the tube coming out of the tank with my eyes all the way up to Sidney's oxygen mask. Three IV bags hung on one pole with two more on another pole on the other side of the bed.

And Sidney, bald and tiny, asleep in the middle of it all. She looked so much worse than the last time I'd seen her in real life. Her sunken eyes had dark rings around them. Her arms looked like they were just bones with no fat or muscle left on them.

Mom pulled on my hand, and we approached. Mr. Thatcher stood on the other side of the bed with a grim expression on his face. Mrs. Thatcher sat next to Sidney's bed, one hand wrapped tightly around Sidney's hand, the other holding a tissue. I noticed Sidney was missing her bracelet. She'd given me the bracelet she had worn as long as I'd known her—the incomplete one, the one she needed to put one more bead on for her very last chemo treatment.

I reached down and touched it on my wrist. I couldn't take this from her. She needed to finish it.

A doctor stepped in the room. "Mr. and Mrs. Thatcher?" He took a quick glance around the room. "Can we speak in the hall?"

Mr. Thatcher nodded and followed the doctor into the hall.

Mrs. Thatcher paused at the door. "Will you stay with her?" she asked.

I nodded, and Mrs. Thatcher gave me a sad smile. "Thank you," she said. She stepped out and shut the door behind her.

"Do you want to be alone with her?" Mom asked. "Or should I stay?"

I was afraid to be alone with her—afraid of death. But I wasn't sure I could say what I wanted to with an audience.

"Can you get me that soda?" I asked.

Mom nodded.

"Thanks." The situation felt surreal.

Mom walked out of the room. And Sidney and I were alone.

I sat down on a rolling circular stool next to Sidney's bed and put my hand on her hand. I had heard people in comas could hear someone talking to them even if they couldn't respond. Was Sidney in a coma or was she sleeping?

"Hey, Sidney. What happened back there?" I rolled closer, careful to not smash any of the cords or tubes lying on the floor.

"I thought you were right behind me. I wouldn't have left without you.

"My mom said you aren't going to make it." A lump rose in my throat. "She said you only have a week." My eyes burned as they filled with fresh tears. "I really want to say..." I swallowed hard. The words stuck on the lump in my throat. I exhaled a shaky breath but it didn't help. Nothing would.

"Everything about this is wrong—we're only eleven. We're not supposed to be sick." The words fell out in a rush and with a sob. I put my head near her arm and let the tears fall.

"You're too young. It's not fair," I sobbed. "I'm so sorry, Sidney. I'm sorry." I let the feelings overwhelm me. I couldn't hold them back anymore. "I'm sorry you're sick. I'm sorry you don't get to have your twelfth birthday. I'm sorry you'll never get married or have kids." I squeezed her hand. "It's not fair! This isn't fair.

"I'm sorry I didn't visit you after the first time you were diagnosed. I was five and scared. But you were also five and going through terrible things. I should have come." I thought of Alexa. "I know now how it feels to have friends abandon you when you're sick."

I closed my eyes, squeezing more tears out. My breaths were coming too fast. I was getting light-headed. I slowed my breathing to match Sidney's machine. "I'm sorry we missed out on so many years of friendship." My voice wavered. "Thanks for not giving up on me." I gave her hand another squeeze ... and she squeezed back.

I sat up and looked at her. One eye cracked open. She squeezed my hand again—so faint I almost didn't feel it.

"You hear me?" I asked.

Another feather-light squeeze.

Looking down at the bracelet Sidney had given me, I made a decision. Sidney needed as much strength as possible right now.

I slid it off my wrist and onto hers. My hand closed around her hand and I whispered, "You need this more than I do right now."

Her hand squeezed mine one more time.

Mr. and Mrs. Thatcher returned, still looking dazed. Mom came in right after them, with a soda for me.

My stomach clenched and I felt dizzy and queasy from my chemo treatment. It must have shown on my face because Mom set the soda down and stepped over to me. "Are you okay?" She put her arm around me.

I shook my head. My skin prickled, feeling both hot and cold at the same time.

Mom grabbed a throw up bag and ushered me out of the room. "You'll let me know if she changes?" Mom asked the Thatchers as she guided me out of Sidney's room.

"Of course," Mrs. Thatcher said.

The hospital smell hit me again and I was grateful for the puke bag.

Chapter 22

The drive home was long, but my bed had never felt so welcoming. I fell asleep almost the moment I closed my eyes.

In Dreamland, the weather was worse than before. I woke up in the observatory again. Rain pounded on the dome. I couldn't fly in this weather. I braved the rain to check on the zipline. It must have broken because instead of a tight wire stretching down into the fog, it sat on the ground. After hurrying back inside and drying my clothes I lay down on the floor, thinking. How could I get to Skull Island?

The dim lights of my star chart comforted me. I tried not to notice the curled edges of the chart or the rust that now covered the telescope stand.

The last time Sidney and I were here together, our plan to trick Mr. Black into letting the kids out of detention had failed. Thinking back made me yearn for the happy times I'd had with Sidney. If only the plan would have worked. Sidney and I could be looking at the stars together right now.

Instead, the search-night had attracted Mr. Blacks attention and we'd had to bail.

I sat up. Could it work twice?

If I could lead Mr. Black to me, I could get to Skull Island.

I hopped up and tried to open the dome with the switch, but it jammed and I had to pry it open. Rain pounded on the observatory floor. The knobs to move the telescope didn't work either. Thankfully, it was still pointed down toward Skull Island. I crossed my fingers and flipped it to Night mode. Seeing the beam of night shoot out of the telescope still gave me a little thrill.

I flew up to the edge of the retracted dome and perched on it until I spotted the black pirate ship. It sailed easily through the rain. When it arrived, I flew down to the ground to meet it.

"Jessa?" Mr. Black said. Rain fell harder as he walked down the ramp

He cocked his head and rubbed his chin. "Have you seen Caroline?"

"I—what? Wait, you're *looking* for Mrs. Black?" I asked.

The temperature dropped and the rain turned to a light snow. He sighed. "I can't find her anywhere. I feel like she's near. Every time I look for her, I find another kid skipping class."

He looked around, seeming almost startled by the now falling snow. "This weather is crazy. It reminds me of Caroline. She loves the snow."

"Mr. Black?"

He turned back toward me. He gave me a puzzled look, like he'd just noticed me for the first time. "Jessa? What are you doing here? Have you seen Caroline?"

"I haven't seen her," I said in the calm voice I used when Kate had a meltdown.

"I haven't seen her, either. Not for quite some time." He deflated.

The snow changed to a downpour, almost like it matched his mood.

"She was my favorite teacher," I said, trying to come up with a plan. "I loved the stories she read to us. *Peter Pan* was her favorite."

Mr. Black's confused eyes focused on me. "Yes. She

reminded me of Mrs. Darling. You know, the part about how she had a hidden kiss in the corner of her mouth. Caroline did." He smiled.

The rain outside stopped.

Wait, was his mood tied to the weather? I wanted to verify it. "You said a lot of kids were skipping class?" Would that make him upset?

His face darkened. "They're not supposed to."

Thunder boomed.

"Would Mrs. Black know what to do about them?" I ventured.

"I can't find her anywhere. What if something terrible happened?" The rain started up again.

I was right. The weather changed with his mood. Was his grief destroying Dreamland? "I might know where she is. Can you take me to Sidney?" My heart pounded in my throat.

He stepped closer coming right up to my face. His eyes were wide and wild. The rain started pouring again. "You've seen Caroline here?"

"Yes." I had forgotten about my very first time in Dreamland. Mrs. Black had been here the night of her funeral. "But you have to take me to Sidney. Then I can help you find her."

"Okay," he agreed.

Together we boarded the cloud ship.

The deck of the ship reminded me of the cloud maze, but the texture seemed more like cotton balls instead of cotton candy. Once we boarded the ship, we flew through the wind, over the snowy beaches and wild ocean, to Skull Island. By the time we landed I had formulated a plan. But I needed Sidney.

Together Mr. Black and I walked down the hall past his classroom. Rafa looked alarmed when he saw us approach. I tried to give him an encouraging smile, but he looked even more worried as we walked past toward the office.

"Come and have a cup of hot chocolate," Mr. Black offered.

I stayed in the doorway of the teachers' lounge. Mr. Black grabbed two mugs from a cupboard.

As I waited, I looked across the hall for Sidney. She lay on the bed. Her eyes widened when she saw me. The glass door I'd smashed was gone and hadn't been replaced. Was Sidney magically stuck in the room like the other kids?

Mr. Black placed a mug in the microwave. "Do you want marshmallows in yours?" He shut the microwave and started it.

"Can Sidney have some too?" I asked. We needed to be together if my plan was going to work.

"Of course," Mr. Black said with a smile. "Hot cocoa is one of Caroline's favorite treats. She always says it's the perfect pick-me-up. I remember in our first apartment..."

"Are you okay?" I whispered to Sidney, as Mr. Black told me a story about the early years of his marriage.

"I'm fine. What are you doing here?" Sidney whispered, as she walked toward me.

I stepped across the hall toward her room. "I needed to get here and I couldn't fly through the storm, so I let him catch me," I whispered back. "I think I know how to fix Dreamland, but I need your help." I moved closer to her.

"You figured out how to help him?" Sidney asked. She stood right on the brink of the doorway.

I nodded toward Mr. Black. "He's looking for his wife. We were right, he doesn't realize he's dreaming. His grief over her is so strong, it's overpowering all the magic here."

Sidney nodded. "What do we do?"

"I think we need to show him Mrs. Black. I can't do it alone, though." I stepped right up to her.

Understanding dawned on Sidney's face. She held her hand

out to me. I could feel her power surge through me. Sidney had lived in this world longer than most of the kids here. And even though she'd gone through years of illness and hardship, she was still a light to everyone around her. The magic lived inside her. And it was stronger than the sadness around her.

Our hands touched, and warmth flowed into me. I focused all of my energy into looking like Mrs. Black.

I knew it worked when Sidney gasped.

Mr. Black pulled an empty mug from the cupboard and turned toward us. The mug slipped from his hand and shattered on the floor though he didn't seem to notice.

"Caroline?" he whispered. "Is it you?" He walked toward me, boots crunching on the shattered glass.

"Jim," I said trying to imitate Mrs. Black's voice. "Why are you keeping all these children?"

"They were skipping class. You wouldn't believe the things they did while I searched for you." He stepped into the hall. "Where have you been?"

"You know I'm gone, Jim. Remember? I had a stroke." I held my hands out to the school around us. "This place is a dream. You're in the hospital."

"What?" He looked alarmed. "What do you mean?"

"You were so sad after I died. You needed help." I tried to remember how Michael had described it. "You had a mental breakdown and they took you to the hospital." I squeezed Sidney's hand.

Mr. Black shot Sidney a suspicious look. "How do I know that's really you?"

Thunder boomed, making my heart race.

The quote Mrs. Black had hanging up in her classroom came into my mind. Hadn't she said it was her favorite? "Shall we make a new rule of life from tonight: always try to be a little kinder than is necessary?"

"Your favorite J. M. Barrie quote," Mr. Black whispered. The howling wind quieted for a moment. He took a step toward me but I held my hand up to stop him.

"Jim, you won't find me here again. You need to go back," I said in Mrs. Black's voice.

"I—I can't," he said, his voice cracking. Tears streamed from his eyes. The wind picked back up and rain pounded on the roof.

The ground shook so hard it made the floor crack.

Sidney let go of my hand and the disguise fell away. Ignoring the earthquake, she took a step toward him. "Mr. Black? She's okay. She's in the most beautiful place." Sidney glanced back at me. Tears filled her eyes and a golden glow surrounded her.

"You don't know that," he shouted at Sidney, though he still looked down at the floor. A bolt of lightning struck the top of Skull Island and several lights outside the room exploded in showers of sparks.

"I do. I've seen it. Your wife is there. She's happy and she wants you to be happy." Sidney sniffed.

The realization of what she said hit me. She had moved beyond Dreamland. Did that mean... I couldn't finish the thought.

Mr. Black's face was contorted with rage and pain. The howling wind increased to a deafening roar so intense I knew a hurricane must be beating down on Skull Island.

I grabbed her hand and pushed all my focus into being Mrs. Black again. "Jim, I'm okay." The words flowed out of my mouth but they hadn't come from me. They weren't even what I had planned to say.

"I don't know how to live without you." His voice shook and the school shook with it.

"Life doesn't always go as planned. You need to make the

best of what you've been given." Again, the words came out different than what I'd planned. Was Mrs. Black somehow speaking through me?

His stark face looked back at me. "I'll always love you."

"And I'll be waiting." Goosebumps shot up my back.

Mr. Black looked at me and I held onto Mrs. Black's appearance as long as I could. His eyes were wide and he had a sad smile on his face. The ground stopped trembling. The wind ceased. Mr. Black flickered, then disappeared.

I dropped her hand and let the disguise fall away.

Sidney and I looked at each other in disbelief.

"I couldn't have done this without you," I said. "Thanks for your help."

"You had a good plan." Sidney gave me a small smile.

We walked into the sixth-grade hall. Doors opened as kids flooded out of the classrooms. Rafa and Lauren walked down the hall and out of the school together.

Sidney and I walked back to the entrance. She took my hand and we flew out of the skull's eyes.

The sun had come out. A beautiful rainbow stretched across the sky. Below us a purple-haired mermaid popped up and waved at us. Dreamland was getting back to normal.

Sidney kept hold of my hand even though we could fly on our own now. I knew where we were going, but I let her lead me there.

When we landed in her meadow, it was more beautiful than before. Colorful butterflies fluttered all around us. We walked through soft grass among hundreds of fragrant wildflowers.

"Wow," I breathed. "I love it here." I grinned widely at Sidney, but she didn't smile back.

Something wasn't right.

"Sidney?"

She looked down at herself—at the golden glow surrounding her.

My insides went cold despite the warm sun. I felt frozen in place. I didn't want to hear what she was going to say.

"Let's fly more," I said, hoping to delay the inevitable.

"I can't." Sidney bent down and picked a few flowers, offering no further explanation.

"Was it true?" I asked. "About seeing Mrs. Black beyond Dreamland?" I knew the answer, but I wanted her to deny it, to tell me she'd made it all up to save the day.

Tears brimmed Sidney's eyes but she smiled. She blinked and they spilled down her cheeks. "Jessa, every word was true."

Words failed me. Sidney stood before me, and I knew this was the last time I'd see her.

"I've got to go back." Sidney took a step forward and touched my shoulder.

"No, please, stay," I begged. My eyes burned with tears; the lump in my throat felt like I'd swallowed a golf ball. "I'm sorry," I cried. "I should have been a better friend."

"Jessa, it's okay. I heard all the things you said to me in the hospital," she whispered. "Why do you think I came back? You needed to know that I forgive you. And I needed to help you fix Dreamland."

"Please don't go," I begged again. "Please. I can't—I'm not ready to do this alone."

Sidney held both my shoulders at arm's length. "Jessa, you won't be alone. Think of all of your family and friends in the real world and here in Dreamland. You healed this place. You saved it. I stayed to help you, but it's time for me to go now."

Tears streamed down my cheeks; my face was wet with them. I sniffed and nodded. "Are you afraid?"

She stepped forward and wrapped me up in a hug. "More

adventures await beyond Dreamland, and adventures are nothing to be afraid of."

A sob escaped my throat and I hugged her back until she gently pushed me away. She handed me the wildflowers she'd picked.

With a huge smile, she said, "I'll meet you there someday."

The air shimmered around her, glowing brighter and brighter until I looked away. A warm breeze blew past.

I opened my eyes as the bright light winked out.

Sidney was gone.

Chapter
23

"Jessa," Mom shook me awake. "Jessa."

My eyes fluttered open. Moonlight streamed in through my blinds. Mom sat on the end of my bed with tears in her eyes and a box of tissues in her hand. I knew what was going on. I knew why she had woken me in the middle of the night.

"*Nena*, I have something to tell you." Her eyes brimmed with tears. She breathed a long, shuttering sigh.

I cut her off. She didn't need to say it. "Sidney is gone."

Mom looked surprised but nodded. "How did you—"

"I just know." My heart was hollow. Sidney was really gone, and I wanted to cry. I wanted to scream and rage at everyone and everything. Instead I sat there, holding Mom's hand, seeing details around me that I'd never noticed before.

My blanket had a small purple stain. Was that nail polish?

The skin on Mom's hands looked cracked around the knuckles. Little black scabs peppered the chapped area.

My favorite stuffed unicorn had a tiny hole in one of its feet.

Why was I thinking about blankets and unicorns and chapped skin? Sidney had *died*. I would never see her again.

I thought back to the last words she said to me. *I'll meet you there someday.*

Another place beyond Dreamland. Could it be true?

I wasn't sure. I had never seen it. But after what I'd seen in

Dreamland, I knew I could trust Sidney. A warmth burned inside me, pushing away my anger.

Somehow, in one of the worst moments of my life, I felt peace. I knew I would miss her tremendously, but I also knew she was happy.

"Are you okay?" Mom asked. She wrapped her arms around me and pulled me into a hug.

"Yes. No." I snuggled into Mom, trying to gather my thoughts. "I don't know. I am sad for me but happy for Sidney."

"She's in a better place now," Mom said.

"I know. She said she'll wait for me there," I whispered.

Mom pulled me away to look at me. "What did you say?" She looked concerned.

"Someday I'll see her again. She'll be waiting." I said.

Like a whisper on the wind, I heard Sidney's voice say, "Come fly with me."

I STOOD in line in my Sunday best. My tights were itchy and my shoes a little too small. I'd lost enough weight from being sick that the new Maxi dress Mom had bought hung loosely around my waist. Mom squeezed one hand, and Kate squeezed the other. The headband Sarah gave me head dug into my bald scalp.

Mr. and Mrs. Thatcher stood next to the small casket, shaking hands with each person in line. Painted butterflies of all colors covered the casket. I smiled, thinking of Sidney's meadow. Her butterflies were much prettier than the paintings on the casket, but she would have loved these just the same.

We took a step forward. I could see part of her bald head. She wore a headband, too.

Now it was our turn to shake hands with the Thatchers.

Mom first. "I'm so sorry."

Mrs. Thatcher pulled her in for a hug and they murmured words of comfort to each other.

When I stepped forward to shake Mrs. Thatcher's hand, she pulled me into a hug too. "Thank you for being Sidney's friend. I know you didn't see each other much, but she talked about you all the time."

"We had our own way of communicating," I said.

Mrs. Thatcher let me out of the hug but held onto one of my hands. "Come here," she said, "I have something for you."

She and I stepped out of the line and walked across the room to her purse. She dug around in it then pulled out a small bag. "Sidney wanted you to have this."

I opened it. Inside, Sidney's beaded bracelet sat on top of a pile of unstrung beads. "Thank you." Hot tears sprang to my eyes but didn't fall.

"Those beads are some of her favorites." She reached in and pulled out a wooden butterfly bead. "She got this one when she rang the bell last time. She used to carry it everywhere with her." She returned the bead and closed up the bag. "She left a space on the bracelet for her last round of treatments this time." She cleared her throat and sniffed. Her voice shook when she spoke. "I hope you'll finish it for her."

I nodded, not trusting my voice. I took her hand and gave it a squeeze. I took a shallow breath before I spoke. "I don't think I'll ever have another friend like her."

Mr. Thatcher came over. His eyes were bloodshot, and his skin was blotchy from crying. "Hannah, the Johnstons are waiting for you." He nodded back at Alexa and her mom standing in the front of the line.

Mrs. Johnston gave me a smile. Her eyes were red-rimmed, and she held a tissue in her hand. Alexa stood behind her. She didn't look at me but it didn't bother me.

"Of course." Mrs. Thatcher squeezed my shoulder. "Take care, will you?"

I nodded and we all walked back to the line. Mom and Kate must have already gone through.

Unlike at Mrs. Black's funeral, this time when my turn came to step up to the casket, I wasn't afraid of what I'd see.

Sidney's hands lay together on her chest holding a bouquet of wildflowers. She wore a pink dress with a matching headband. A beaded necklace lay around her neck. She looked stiff and cold.

This was her body, but it wasn't her. The Sidney I remembered had short, spiky, brown hair and a contagious smile. She liked to dive off tree houses and fly into the sky. She loved playing racing games and almost always won. The chocolate ice cream fruit was her favorite. And her most special place was a meadow covered with flowers and butterflies. *That* Sidney was off playing beyond even Dreamland. And I knew she was okay.

Chapter
24

Snow fell lightly. The bell rang for lunch and the class crowded to the door. Winter break started tomorrow, and I couldn't wait, though I'd miss my new friends. I had been back to school for two weeks and Mom only let me go part time. I had to go home after lunch.

My locker jammed, and I spent several minutes trying to open it. Finally, it popped open and I shoved my books inside and headed to the lunchroom. They were all at lunch already. They always got there first. And I'd have to sit on the end and miss most of the fun.

The crowded hall seemed busier than normal. Someone bumped into me, and I stumbled.

"Oh, I'm sorry," Alexa said.

"No problem."

"How have you been?" Her eyes darted up to the wisps of hair starting to grow back on my head.

I shrugged. "Good, I guess." I could tell she wanted to ask about my treatments but wasn't sure how. I wanted to roll my eyes at her. Instead, I saved her from awkwardness and responded to the question she hadn't asked. "I finished chemo a few weeks ago, and I'm almost done with radiation." I fingered Sidney's bracelet—I could put the last bead on tonight.

"That's good," she said. We started walking to the lunch room together. "We should hang out."

We walked through the lunchroom doors together and

typed in our numbers for the lunch lady. "Yeah, I'd like that," I said looking around for my friends.

Michael jumped up and called my name. "Jessa, I saved you a spot."

Alexa grabbed her tray and gave Michael a skeptical look. "Do you want to eat lunch with us today? The other girls won't mind." She glanced back at Michael and the rest of the kids at his table. It was the usual assortment of our friends who didn't fit into any of the cliques but always fit together—some from band, some from chess club, a few kids with colorful hair and dramatic makeup.

The lunch workers filled my tray with food and we moved to the silverware station.

"I'm okay, thanks. They already saved me a seat." I grabbed a stack of napkins. Michael was the messiest eater I'd ever encountered, and he never grabbed enough.

Alexa cocked her eyebrow. "Are you sure?"

I looked over at Carleigh and Anna, then back to my usual table. "Yeah. I'm good, but you can join us, if you'd like."

"Alexa, hurry up!" Carleigh shouted across the lunch room.

Alexa acknowledged her with a wave. "Maybe another time?"

"Sure." I walked across the lunch room and sat down next to Michael.

After Sidney died, Michael had come to visit at least once a week. When I came back to school, I started eating lunch with him. His group of friends had welcomed me with open arms. They didn't shun me when I was bald or make excuses as to why they couldn't come visit me when I was sick. They reminded me of the kids in Dreamland.

A few of the kids were in the middle of a rousing milk drinking contest. The kids who weren't participating did their best to make the milk-drinkers laugh.

One heckler succeeded and milk sprayed across the table. We all burst into laughter.

Mr. Black walked past without a glance at us. He'd taken a few months off and had intensive therapy. Mom said he needed to work through his grief, and I understood. We'd never spoken about Dreamland. Perhaps adults didn't remember their time there...but once in a while he'd look at me differently. As though we had shared something.

AFTER SCHOOL we drove up for my last treatment and the whole family came with me.

The whole time we sat in the waiting room, the kids' phone buzzed with Michael's usual texts. He'd made everything more bearable. Mom said he was a much better influence than Alexa, and I agreed.

I read Michael's latest text and laughed. I handed the phone to Dad. "Read this one."

Dad read Michael's text out loud: "Would soup with substance be called soupstance?" His eyes widened and he smiled. "Brilliant. I like this kid."

Mom and Sarah laughed along with us.

I took the phone back from Dad. **Dad loved it**, I wrote back.

Because I'm awesome, Michael wrote.

I sent back a few eye-roll emojis.

Three dots appeared while he typed his next message. **Are you almost done?**

I think I'm next, I wrote.

Have your mom take a video when you ring the bell.

Will do, I responded.

I gotta go. Mom's calling me for dinner.

Are you having soupstance? I asked.

My favorite. :)

The nurse took me back to the radiation room and set me up on the table. As always, I held as still as I could as she pushed the buttons—it felt no worse than getting an X-ray, though I always felt achy after.

When she finished, she walked me back to the radiology waiting area. Together, my family and I walked down the hall to oncology. Dad stopped and studied Lauren's map of Dreamland in the hall.

"I was here as a child," he said, "at this hospital. When I got that virus I told you about."

"You said you played a lot of Space Invaders," I reminded him. "Where did you play it?"

Dad continued to stare at the picture. "The arcade," he said absently. "I think."

I smiled. Would he remember if I told him? "Come on, Dad," I tugged on his arm. "Let's go."

Several nurses stood, waiting for me. My nurse nudged another worker. "This is my favorite part."

They smiled and sang me a song. One of my favorite nurses read the poem. Everyone fell silent as I walked up to the cancer bell. My chest felt tight with emotion.

I grabbed the small rope and rang the bell.

Once, twice, three times.

Everyone clapped.

Dad videoed me. Mom wiped her watery eyes, and Sarah pulled her into a side hug. Kate's smile warmed my heart. While the nurses talked and laughed with my parents, I pulled out Sidney's bag of beads.

I dug around with my fingers until I found the butterfly bead. I sat down in one of the chairs and untied the string. Carefully, I pulled a few beads off so I could put the butterfly where it would look best. When I finished, I smiled and slid it back on my wrist.

Dreamland was back to normal. I visited both my observatory and Sidney's meadow every time. I would fly up to the clouds, then dive in spirals back down to the earth. I knew my time there was coming to an end. Last night I'd had a regular dream for the first time since Mrs. Black's funeral.

I'd miss the arboretum and the game room. I'd miss the library and the lava hot chocolate springs. I'd miss flying wherever I wanted to go. But the best part of Dreamland wasn't in Dreamland anymore.

I missed her every day. But someday, I knew, I'd see her again.

Author's Note

I have felt passionately about childhood cancer ever since my sister fought Hodgkin Lymphoma when we were both teens. My sister survived, but a few years ago I was struck hard when a thirteen-year-old cancer patient I'd been rooting for passed. Before her death, this fighter sang a haunting song about Neverland. A few months after her passing, Jessa and Sidney's story came together, the words pouring out.

As I wrote this book, both of these cancer warriors--one who survived and one who didn't--were in my mind and heart. I wanted to portray hope and healing for anyone who might be going through cancer or knows someone who is. I also understood the reality that not all cancer warriors win the fight. I wanted to honor both groups in the story I told.

To the children reading this story: Sometimes you might feel small and think you can't change anything in the world because you aren't an adult yet. You don't need to do anything big like make a video or write a book to make a difference. You have the ability to change the lives of those around you just by being a kind and empathetic friend like Sidney. To see how you can help children with cancer, ask your parent or guardian to call your local children's hospital and see what they need. It doesn't have to cost money. The best gifts are from the heart.

To the adults reading this story: For more information on childhood cancer, here are some of my favorite websites: thetruth365.org, stjude.org, curechildhoodcancer.org

There are many ways to serve and help that don't cost a lot of money. The best place to start is your local children's hospital.

Acknowledgments

This book wouldn't have been possible without the help of many people. Thank you to Chandler for all the support you've given me over the years. From writing conferences and retreats to reading this book multiple times (and even writing a scene when I couldn't), this book could not have happened without you. I love you.

Thanks to Emily for letting me read the whole book to her one long Sunday afternoon and giving me great feedback. I hope to return the favor to you someday with your own book. Thanks to Patrick for all the times I needed a writing break. Playing soccer in the front yard usually did the trick.

My amazing beta readers, Jenny Hahn, Caren Hahn, Ivory Hahn, Sterling Whipple, Becky Jensen, and Vicki Jackman, thank you for taking the time to read this. The feedback you gave made the book better than I could have made it on my own.

I had a bit of research to do for the medical side of this book. Anything that is right about this is thanks to Becky Holman, Sterling Whipple, Jessica Garcia, Katie Hensley, Vicki Jackman, Becky Jensen, and Nick Whipple. Thank you for taking the time to answer my questions, share your experiences, and make corrections.

Thanks to Chandler Whipple and Ana Nelson for help with all the Spanish words and phrases.

A big thanks to Lisa Mangum. Thank you for helping me with my query letter, synopsis, and answering all the random questions I've had. You've been an amazing resource for how things work in the publishing world.

I'm especially grateful for my amazing critique group, Sarah

Alva, Stacy Codner, Emily Huey, Apryl Lopez, and Miranda Renae who have stuck with me for ten years. We've grown together as writers and as people. You have turned into some of my best friends and closest confidants. Thank you. This book would not have happened without your feedback and encouragement.

A huge thank you to all the people at Immortal Works who have worked on this book to make it better. Rachel Huffmire and Holli Anderson, thank you for taking a chance on this story and helping make my dream of publishing a reality. Thanks also to Audrey Hammer. Your meticulous editing and fantastic eye for the storyline helped me take this story to the next level. I'm grateful for your amazing suggestions.

About the Author

Julie Hahn grew up in a small town in central Utah. When she was ten, she fell in love with reading and used it as a way to both escape and confront her fears and worries. She believes that books can help everyone deal with hard issues in safe ways.

She was blessed to meet her husband and best friend in high school. They now live in Salt Lake City with their wonderful children and three crazy cats. When she's not writing, you'll find her working in kindergarten at a local elementary school or crocheting animals for her kids.

This has been an
Immortal Production